11-6-04

E. J.

I hope you like this weird story. Thank you and best wishes

Bill

SIN CITY

G.W. Reynolds III

In writing these true stories, it was necessary to change the names of the children. As educators, we are all charged with protecting the children. That's what we do.

Dr. G.W. Reynolds has been an educator for 29 years. He has served as a teacher, coach, and administrator. His doctoral research at the University of North Florida and his experiences with prenatal drug exposed children, prompted him to write Sin City. Dr. Reynolds offers these stories as a tribute to all educators and an introduction for the public to the real world of those educators.

Published and Distributed by
RIVER CITY PRESS

For more information, write or call:
River City Press
9880-3 San Jose Blvd.
Jacksonville, FL 32257
904 730-0571
Contact G.W. Reynolds at www.jettyman.com

Dedication

To all the elementary school teachers who go far beyond the formal call of duty by staying late, drying tears, wiping noses, tying shoelaces, protecting, and caring about the child's first steps on their educational journey.

To the middle school and junior high teachers who go the extra mile by listening, counseling, directing and introducing the students to the life lessons they will need in the future.

To the high school teachers who wake-up early, stay late, sponsor activities, become involved in the future of their students, and prepare our young adults for the complexities of life in our society.

IF YOU STILL SUCK YOUR THUMB
YOU SHOULDN'T GIVE THE FINGER.

Prelude

We left Jacksonville Beach as Sedro's burgundy Pontiac Star Chief rolled across the Intracoastal Waterway Bridge on Atlantic Boulevard. Our destination was the Saturday night dance at the Southside Woman's Club. *Mouse, the Boys and Brass*, would be the band playing our favorite tunes and the place would be packed with beautiful young ladies from all parts of the city. The four of us were already excited about being together and we were ready for an eventful evening and even more excitement to come. I was in the back seat with Bobby Woolard. Sedro was driving, it was his car, and Don Day was in the passenger's side up front. Don always seemed to be in the front seat. He also seemed to have the more interesting ideas and suggestions.

"Before we go to the dance let's go to Sin City. Ya'll know about Sin City, don't ya?"

Now, we had all heard of Sin City, but hadn't given it much thought. Don had more to challenge us. "If we stay on Atlantic we'll pass right by the turn-off for Sin City. They got real women walking the streets lookin' for men to buy sex. They come right up to the cars." Sedro nodded his head as if he knew what Don was talking about. I looked at Bobby. His eyes were opened wide after Don's comment. Bobby always had something funny to say.

"Kinda like the way the waitresses come to the car window at the A&W Drive-In, huh?" Don shook his head. He didn't think Bobby's comment was funny. I thought it was.

Sedro was ready. "Let's go. Show me where to turn."

We were on our way to Sin City, the red light district where painted ladies of the evening walked the streets in search of men willing to pay for their sexual favors. To see such a sight would be true adventure for four teenagers in the 1960's. In a matter of minutes Don pointed out a street and directed Sedro to make the turn into the notorious area called Sin City.

Sedro drove slowly and we all looked out the window on our side of the car into the darkness of the poorly lighted streets, hoping to make contact with the legendary sexual wonders. What we saw was true southern poverty, dirty children out too late at night, pit bulls barking from behind chicken wire fences and darkness. It was a darkness I was sure never lifted.

We saw no painted ladies and only one light in a window, but it wasn't red, it was blue. We had no idea what that meant. Our attempt to have a sexual adventure was just that, an attempt. All four of us acted disappointed, but as I look back we were all probably relieved we hadn't encountered the forbidden world. We went on to the dance and I never thought much more about Sin City as my life continued. I had no idea on that night that twenty years later I would be the principal of an elementary school in the middle of Sin City, a neighborhood lost in time.

The Bird and The Word

Maurice sat in my office and stared at me, as usual, with his jet black eyes surrounded by snow-white corneas. He was a beautiful black child. He had the most perfectly round shaped head I had ever seen. His skin tone was perfect like his head. Maurice was definitely too little and too handsome to be such big and ugly trouble. He had only been on Earth for five years and even more significant, he had only been in kindergarten for six weeks. In that short amount of time he had found his calling, disruption. Already that morning, Maurice had kicked a number of classmates, thrown crayons across the room, spit on his teacher and torn pages from his picture book. He had broken as many rules as possible in the first hour of the school day, but he had colored a picture perfectly, never going out of the lines.

Maurice was a strange little boy. There was no doubt he was a crack baby. Crack cocaine had been in our city for about seven or eight years and Maurice was the right age to be one of the first casualties who had been exposed to the drug while in his mother's womb. Educators would see many children who suffered from pre-natal exposure to cocaine in the years that followed.

Maurice had the face of an angel, but it was difficult to see his handsome features most of the time. He was a serious thumb sucker and that little thumb of his was always stuck in his mouth. His little closed fist was always pressed against his lips. Maurice was tired of seeing me and I was tired of seeing him. But there we sat once again, like two old friends or perhaps old enemies with nothing left to talk about.

The five year old had the unusual ability of staring at you without looking away or blinking. I contributed his ability to do so to his drug exposure. I really didn't like that particular attribute because he always made me look away first. I felt like he was Davy Crockett and I was the bear. As the adult in the situation I just couldn't stand being eyeballed like that and as the principal of the school, I disliked it even more. I wanted to shave Maurice's head to see if maybe he had a birthmark with numbers on it. If so, I would at least know what I was up against and I would be able to call in a member of the clergy. I was sure I had said it many times before, but it just came out of my mouth again.

"I'm so tired of you acting mean to your nice teacher and your nice classmates. I haven't paddled anyone this year and I have never paddled a kindergartner, but if you don't stop acting like this, you will be the first."

His expression didn't change. In fact, I had to take a closer look to see if he was still awake. Some people can sleep with their eyes open and I had no doubt Maurice had that capability as well. I wasn't finished with the five year old.

"I'm going to call your mother again and ask her to come and get you. She can take you home for the rest of the day. Maybe she will spank you when she gets here, so I won't have to use my paddle on you."

As I turned and reached for the phone, I saw a slight movement from Maurice out of the corner of my eye. I looked back quickly and I was greeted by an incredible "Maurice moment". As he still sucked his thumb, Maurice had lifted the middle finger on his closed fisted hand in defiance. What a sight to behold. He stuck that little middle finger of his up in front of his nose, giving me "the finger." He had never stopped sucking his thumb. I felt it took excellent coordination and courage to do such a thing. I also thought it was the first time it had ever been done. Maurice and I were sharing a first. It was a sad first, but a true moment of male "bonding". The combination of thumb sucking innocence and the corruption of the middle finger had no place in the mind and actions of a five-year-old child.

Maurice was still just a baby, but he already had knowledge of the defiant "bird". I wondered if he understood the true meaning behind the upraised middle digit. At first I wanted to grab that little bird and break it as a lesson against future flights, but that was only a gut reaction to Maurice's unexpected show of disrespect. Maurice had given me my first push of the day and my fall from the edge had begun. I really felt deep in my heart, that if you still sucked your thumb you shouldn't "shoot birds" or even know about those kinds of nasty defiant symbols. I talked to his mother on the telephone and I told her about his improper classroom behavior. I didn't say much to her when she came to get him. I was just glad he was gone.

The encounter with Maurice had really bothered me. It was not like me to ponder such things. I decided to visit the cafeteria where one could always find excitement. I figured since I hadn't paddled Maurice I could put the noisy cafeteria crowd on "silence". The principal has the authority to do that.

I was very disappointed when I walked into the lunchroom and found the noise level acceptable and the students seemed to be enjoying their cheese pizza, grilled cheese, cheese fries, and macaroni and cheese lunchtime selections. I knew my arrival had filled them with fear and the, "here comes Mr. Reynolds" syndrome. The teacher's assistant on cafeteria duty, however, put a hole in my fear of the principal theory when she told me the students had been very well behaved during the entire lunch period. I nodded and smiled, but didn't believe her. I couldn't help but feel in my heart that they were being good because the principal was near.

As I walked among the tables, talking to the children, Maurice and his defiant little middle finger left my thoughts. Children were always a remedy for the "blues." Sometimes I talked to children for medicinal purposes. I sat down with our Emotionally Handicapped students. That was a sure way to clear one's head if needed. Nelson spit the majority of his sugar cookie on me when I sat down next to him. He was excited about my choice of seats and was just trying to say hello. I knew the cookie shower was unintentional and I overlooked it. We did discuss "not talking with a mouth full of food", but I am sure I was the only one listening.

David gave me a spaghetti handprint on the sleeve of my white shirt. Again, it was unintentional, but it was still very annoying. You don't just brush off a spaghetti handprint. They usually last all day and sometimes forever. Shirts have been thrown away because of a spaghetti handprint.

Tina made fun of my tie and Nino said I had "skinny lizard" shoes, what ever that was. Nino's observation changed the quiet noise level, and the whole table burst into loud, spontaneous laughter. Evidently, I was the only one at the table who didn't understand the skinny lizard shoe comment. I guess it was my fault for wearing those shoes, so no punishment of silence was inflicted on the children. It was all right for me to cause a disturbance. I was the principal.

I really wanted to stay and continue the fellowship I was enjoying with the abusive, yet funny class. I felt, however, my administrative assistance was needed in other areas of the school. As I moved toward the exit stairs, a tater-tot hit the wall near me and bounced off the top of one of my skinny lizard shoes. I looked up to see at least fifty little fingers pointing in the direction of a first grade girl, Janella.

Now, I recognized Janella right away because that was not the first time she had bounced food off of the cafeteria wall. I knew when our eyes met the fifty fingers were not lying. The true culprit had been rightly identified. The flying tot had come from Janella.

My visit to the cafeteria had been so pleasant that I wasn't really too upset with Janella. The pressure of fifty pairs of eyes, however, waiting for Janella's fate, was too much for me. So to my later sorrow, I added to the confrontation. I should have left it alone. Our eyes were locked together. I began the war of words.

"Why did you throw that?" Janella gave me her version of the Maurice stare-down. I had stared Janella down once before so my confidence level was higher at that time. I had to continue. "I am so tired of you making a mess at lunch. When are you going to stop throwing food and making such a mess?" Janella didn't answer, but she did look away and broke the stare-down. I had used my own style of the "Davy Crocket eyeballing technique" and I was rather proud when the first grader crumbled. Unbelievably, Janella made an incredible recovery when I told her to pick up her lunch tray, move to another table and sit away from her class. Janella turned her head away from me and with two words she ruined my day.

"Fuck you." Those two awful words came from Janelle's six-year-old lips. My throat went dry as she defiantly turned her black eyes back to face me again. A new stare had captured me. There was a faint gasp in stereo from the students sitting at the table, but it only lasted for a few seconds. The table became silent as eyes popped wide and mouths dropped open. Everyone within hearing distance, including me, was in a state of shock. At that moment I made another mistake. It was definitely the biggest mistake of that day. Perhaps it was the mistake of the decade.

"What did you say to me?" It came out of my mouth before I thought about the question. Twenty little voices answered for Janella.

"She said, 'Fuck you,' Mr. Reynolds." I couldn't believe I had given a table full of first graders the go ahead to use the dreaded "F" word for all in the cafeteria to hear. It rolled off their tongues as if they were saying "good morning." Janella joined the push Maurice had started. My fall from the edge continued. I knew it was time to do something to save the children. I just wasn't sure how to do that nor if

I was the one to do it. Maurice and Janella had set the stage for the rest
of that week and the rest of the year.

Love and An Ear

A day later we found out we had a pregnant fifth grader. She was twelve years old and two years behind on grade level. Our guidance counselor, Mrs. McWilliams, had been trying to help the young girl catch up to her proper grade. She was too old and mature to be in the fifth grade and now she was with child. Our concern grew when we met the child's father and he told us the father of the baby was the girl's fifteen-year-old cousin. The information was disturbing enough, but her father made the sad situation even more bizarre when he told us how happy the family was about the baby. It would mean more money coming into the household each month from the government. I called the HRS and turned the family over to the authorities.

There was another sad situation that week when we learned one of our second grade boys had been beaten by his father at home with a guitar string and then placed into a bathtub full of water and ice cubes to keep down the swelling on his body. We called the police and the abuse registry.

On Wednesday morning I had a wisdom tooth pulled and didn't arrive at school until about 10:30. I should have taken the day off and it didn't take very long for me to wish I had. A woman I recognized as one of our parents ran into the office area screaming and holding her hand against the bloody side of her head. I heard her scream and met her at the door of my office.

"Help me, Mr. Reynolds, please help me!" I helped her move to a chair in my office and she sat down as she continued to rant. "My husband's coming to take my children from the school." She seemed ready to faint. The woman was bleeding heavily from her left ear. I asked Mrs. Highsmith, a member of our office staff, to call a rescue unit. Another member of the staff, Ms. Gilmer handed me a wet towel and I wiped some of the blood away so I could see how serious the injury was and where all the blood was coming from. She calmed down as I held the wet towel against the side of her head.

"I'm Jane Holland. My children are Cindy and John. Don't worry about me, please. Just hide my children. My husband's crazy and he's even worse when he's drinkin'. He's comin' to get them. He hit me with a pipe when I told him he couldn't take the children. Please hide them for me."

I continued cleaning the blood away as she talked. I could see that the top of her ear had been torn off and the heavy flow of blood was from the severed ear. As usual, Mrs. McWilliams and the office staff reacted efficiently to the serious situation. They called the police and the rescue unit and the two children were taken to a safe place in the school.

I continued to apply pressure to her injury, hoping to stop the bleeding. The damage to her ear looked serious to me and I was afraid for her. I was also worried about meeting the pipe-swinging husband who could show up at any minute. I hadn't been told about such situations in the administrative classes I had taken in college. As I continued to try and remember my first-aid training, another woman entered my office. She was Ms. Holland's friend, who wanted to take her to the hospital. Ms. Holland stood up, took the blood soaked towel from me, and pressed it against her ear.

"I'll go with her before I bleed to death. Don't let him take my children. Give them to the police when they come." She left my office, rushed to a waiting car and as fast as she had arrived, she was gone.

I agreed with the part about her going to the hospital before she bled to death. My attempt to stop the bleeding had not been successful. I didn't like having the responsibility of hiding her children. Educators are asked to do too much sometimes. I knew I would protect the children, but it was still difficult. It couldn't have been more than three minutes later, when a man walked into the back entrance of the main office. He was very calm and introduced himself.

"I'm John Holland. I'd like to sign my two children out early today, John and Cindy. John's in Ms. Frye's kindergarten class and Cindy's in the third grade, but I don't know her teacher's name."

I was standing in the office, anticipating his arrival, so I stepped up to the counter that separated us. My heart was pounding in my chest as I took a deep breath. It was my job. I was the principal.

"Mr. Holland, your wife was just here, sir. She was really hurt and she said you were the one who hurt her." Mr. Holland's eyes widened after my statement.

"And, that's your business?" His eyes showed his anger.

"Actually, no sir, it's not my business. But, the safety of the children in this school is my business and I don't think this situation is very safe for anyone at the moment." I tried not to show him how nervous I was, but I don't think I was very good at hiding the fact I was as nervous as any human could be. He was glaring at me and he was mad.

"Are you gonna give me my kids or not? I know they're still here. I saw her leave without 'em." I was glad the counter separated us. It helped me be a little braver than I really wanted to be.

"No sir. I'm not. I can't. You can discuss it with the police when they get here."

My heart pounded harder as I visualized the pipe swinging at my head. I was concerned that an ugly confrontation was about to take place at my expense. I wasn't sure what I was going to do so I just stood there waiting for Mr. Holland to take us to the next level of the scary and awkward moment. I would have to decide what to do as things unfolded. As long as the counter was between us, I knew I would have time to run if I felt it was necessary.

As I was preparing to react to what was to come, Mr. Holland helped me with my dilemma. I couldn't believe my eyes when I watched him turn away from the counter and walk back out of the back door. At first I didn't understand his sudden retreat, then I saw a Jacksonville police car pass the office window as it pulled up to the front of the school. Mr. Holland must have seen it too, which explained his hasty retreat. I knew it hadn't been my intimidating presence. The police took the children and went to find Mrs. Holland at the hospital. I spent the rest of the day worried that Mr. Holland would return with his pipe.

Cindy and John continued attending school with us for about another month and then they moved away. I did see Mr. and Mrs. Holland on one other occasion when they picked the children up after school. I guess true love is worth an ear. Were people crazy or what?

I knew Thursday of that week had to be better than the other three days. I also knew my heart and nerves had handled all they could take so far that week. I wished someone had warned me to "Stay home. There will be much more to come."

A Tooth With Little Wisdom

Most of the office talk the next morning was about the excitement and the incident that happened Wednesday. We were all very proud of the way the serious incident had been handled. Mrs. Gilmer, our bookkeeper, made the comment: "We're at our best in a crisis situation. That's the sign of a good staff."

She was right. Anyone can be successful when things are going smoothly. It's the way you handle the serious problems that makes heroes. I was working with a staff of heroes and I was proud to be with them. Successful individuals are only as good as the people around them. I was fortunate to have very competent professionals supporting me.

As we were discussing the moments of the crisis, a fourth grade teacher, Ms. Biggs, called the office on the intercom. Her voice sounded stressed and she requested my immediate assistance.

"Please ask Mr. Reynolds to come to my room. We need help with a disruptive student." The sound of the desks being turned over and children screaming came clearly through the office speaker. I ran to the room.

Upon entering the classroom I saw a student whom I knew as Timmy, standing on one side of the room. The other twenty-five students were all huddled together in another part of the room. Ms. Biggs was standing in a protective stance with the other students wide-eyed behind her. Most of the desks in the room had been turned over. Books and sheets of paper were scattered all over the floor. It looked like a battleground. I could tell Ms. Biggs was relieved to see me as she remained between Timmy's rage and his intimidated classmates.

"He's going to hurt these children, Mr. Reynolds. I don't know what happened to make him act like this, but I can't deal with this." She was more than right. As a teacher, Ms. Biggs should not have to deal with such a situation. Society expects far too much from our educators without even knowing what actually happens each day in our schools. Timmy wasn't looking at me so I had to get his attention. I was worried about how he would react to my being there.

"Timmy, come with me, now." Timmy surprised me when he turned and walked out of the classroom. He had a strange and wild look in his eyes, but he did walk with me. We did not talk as we walked to my office. When we entered my office I told Timmy to sit down. He didn't. He stared out the window, but he didn't sit down.

"Timmy, please sit down and tell me what has happened to make you so mad." He would not talk and remained standing. Mrs. McWilliams walked into my office to offer her assistance.

"Mr. Reynolds, may I help in some way? I know Timmy. He can be a very nice boy. I heard what happened and I'm sure something has happened to make him act like this." Guidance counselors always talk like that. It was part of the counselor's job to make everybody feel better. Mrs. McWilliams was an expert at being calm and finding the right words to calm others, including me. It was my good fortune she was part of the situation.

"Please call Timmy's mother and ask her to come to school." At that point, Timmy attempted to leave the office. Mrs. McWilliams stepped in front of Timmy and blocked his exit. After his aggressive actions in the classroom we had to think of the safety of the staff and the other students. Mrs. McWilliams knew we could not allow him to leave the office. Timmy pulled his arm back and made a threatening motion indicating that he would hit Mrs. McWilliams if she didn't move. I was able to reach Timmy as Mrs. McWilliams stood in his way at the door. I grabbed Timmy and held his arms down. With one movement, Timmy threw his head back and butted me in the jaw with the back of his head. As soon as he hit me I knew the stitches in my mouth had broken loose where my wisdom tooth had just been extracted. It was as if an electric shock had gone through my head. I was hurt and angry as I struggled to hold on to the aggressive child. Timmy tried to hit, kick, bite and head butt me again.

Mrs. McWilliams, realizing my pain after seeing the blood in my mouth, called for more assistance from the office staff. Mrs. Highsmith joined us and the two ladies were able to take Timmy away from me and hold him on the floor as I used first aid on myself. I applied pressure to the wound and tried to stop the bleeding. The ladies were still holding Timmy down on the floor when his mother arrived. His mother agreed it would be better to get him away from school so she could deal with what ever was bothering him. He was suspended until his mother could come back at a later date to discuss the serious problems we were having with him at school.

Bloody Pitchfork

When Friday finally arrived, it was most welcome. I was mentally and physically drained from the events of the week. If there was really such a thing as being on the edge, I seemed to be in that condition rather often. It was a relief that the day was somewhat uneventful in comparison to the other four days of that week. It had been a good day for your average educator, that is, until it was ending.

I had to wait with a first grader who was not picked up after dismissal time at the end of the school day. The child's mother had called and was on her way. I sat and waited with the little boy for about thirty minutes until his mother finally drove up to the front of the school to pick him up. She was very apologetic about being late and thanked me for staying with her son. It didn't bother me that she was late. All I wanted to do was get home and put the crazy week behind me. After they drove away I locked up the school and began walking toward my car in the parking lot. I guess deep down, I knew the calm of the day was too good to be true, but at that point I didn't think anything could surprise me. I was dead wrong with that naive assumption. I actually thought I was dreaming when I looked in the direction from where I heard a strange noise.

It is difficult to explain what I saw. A tall, lanky, bearded man who was wearing a tank top shirt, camouflage pants and calf high, black lace up boots, was standing next to my old, Navy blue, rusty Volkswagen Beetle. He was killing a big dog with a pitchfork. The strange looking man was talking out loud as he stuck the yelping dog with the long steel prongs of the pitchfork. I couldn't hear what the big man was saying. I stepped back to refocus, hoping my eyes were playing tricks on me. It was not a dream and there were no tricks. A dog was being pitch forked to death in the school parking lot and I was watching it happen.

As I stood frozen, not really knowing what to do, or perhaps not wanting to know, a woman stepped out from behind my car. She looked familiar to me. The dog was no longer making any noise. The man stopped. The dog was dead. The woman walked toward me. Her southern accent rang in my ears.

"Mr. Reynolds, my husband just killed that dawg. What do ya want him to do with it?" I was shocked with her question and even more shocked with my answer.

"Yes I know. I just watched him kill it. I didn't kill it, ma'am. You do something with it." I didn't know where that statement came from and I still didn't know what to say or do. That's what happens when you are in a state of shock. The man took a few steps toward the woman. Unfortunately, she was standing close to me. I heard my heart beating as he approached me. I had to say something.

"Please sir, stay over there. Bloody pitchforks really make me nervous." I couldn't believe the man smiled as if he thought I was joking. Perhaps he enjoyed my obvious fear. Some folks like to see fear in others. He kept his strange grin.

"I wouldn't hurt you, Mr. Reynolds." His grin was even bigger and he seemed to bathe in my discomfort. I wasn't curious and I didn't care, but he wanted me to know more. "That damn dog's been killin' our ducks and chickens and I finally got 'im, good. Can I use your dumpster?"

"Sure" was all I could say.

He turned and walked back to the dead dog, took the pitchfork and stuck the prongs back into the bloody carcass lifting it off the ground. He walked to the dumpster at the edge of the parking lot and shook the dead dog off the end of the pitchfork. It disappeared as it dropped into the metal dumpster. While he was at the dumpster, I moved quickly past the woman and got into my car. I fired up my old bug and drove out of the parking lot. I wasn't sure if I could cope with returning on Monday, but for some reason I would. Were people crazy, or what?

P.T.A. Nightmare

I had serious reservations about the capabilities of our new Parent, Teacher Association board members. The school seemed to have problems keeping an active P.T.A. through an entire school year. We would always start each year with great expectations, but something would happen and the organization would crumble. I guess I should have been happy when two of our parents asked to create a new P.T.A. One of the ladies seemed very capable and presentable, while the other one was very strange and un-kempt in her appearance. I wasn't sure how I could go to the P.T.A President and Principal Luncheon at the end of the year with the slovenly member of the P.T.A. I understood she was poor. I've known people who were poor, but they were clean. Due to the lack of parental support and interest, various members of the staff and I had been the P.T.A. for that year. I was pleased when the two ladies took the additional burden off my shoulders. Perhaps the dirty woman would surprise me and take a bath before the luncheon in May.

The two women wanted to have a Halloween Carnival as the major fundraiser for the year. Even though I knew our past luck with such activities had not been very good, they deserved a chance to try. They were excited and I tried not to judge the present project because of past bungles. Preparations for the event got underway and things seemed to be progressing nicely. As usual, a number of complaints about celebrating Halloween forced us to change the name from the "Halloween Carnival" to "October Festival", but that was no big deal.

Then, early in the morning, about ten minutes before the pledge to the flag, it happened. I should have known it was all too good to be true. To me it would always be the "P.T.A. Nightmare".

Mrs. McWilliams and I were sitting in my office talking about the sad death of her cat over the weekend. She just didn't know how Fluffy could have gotten into the clothes dryer at home. She thought the thumping noise she was hearing was a pair of her daughter's tennis shoes bouncing around in the dryer. Evidently, it turned out to have been Fluffy. She also thought she had heard the cat meowing somewhere in the house. After the third or fourth thump of what she thought was tennis shoes, the meowing stopped. As she was telling me the incredible and sad story, Mrs. McWilliams looked out the office window toward the front yard of the school. I noticed it right away when a strange expression came over her face. I didn't know if she was thinking about the death of her cat, but there was a moment of silence as she gazed out the window. She broke the short moment of silence.

"Mr. Reynolds, look out the window and see if you see what I see." It was an unusual request and I wasn't sure I wanted to look at all. Like the curious fool I am, I stood up and moved away from my desk so I could see out the window. Another riveting sight captivated me. It had to be a dream, or a nightmare I was having during the day. I'm not sure what type of moment Mrs. McWilliams and I were sharing. I did know the vision would be etched in our minds forever.

The unclean P.T.A. lady was out in the front yard of the school choking the cleaner P.T.A. lady. They were both stretched out over the small rounded hood of a car, my car. They were pulling each other's hair and punching and kicking one another in a tag-team fury. It was a P.T.A. member's brawl in the parking lot for all to see. I ran outside hoping to stop the battle. As I approached the warriors they looked like a couple of fighting roosters in a ring. There was a pair of crutches on the ground next to my car and I could see a bandaged foot as the kicking continued. The two women rolled off the hood of my car and fell to the ground. They clawed and punched each other in the dirt and pine needles beneath the pine trees by the parking lot. It was absolutely amazing.

They were like two out of breath gladiators when I separated them. The separation was short lived as they slammed back together and fell to the ground again. Neither woman was very clean at that point. Then the original unclean woman picked up one of the crutches, not for support, but to use as a weapon. I had to get involved so no one would be seriously injured. I grabbed the crude weapon and separated them again. They were tired as I pulled them apart and it was obvious they were ready to end the physical altercation and ridiculous spectacle.

"You two stop or I'm calling the police. What's wrong with you two? Now stop." They were like children as I stood between them so I treated them as such. "Both of you go inside to my office. Everybody's watching you and you are embarrassing the school and your children."

To my surprise they both walked with me to the office. The unclean woman was the one who needed the crutches. The clean lady walked ahead as I waited for the other. I will never forget the looks the two women and I received from Mrs. McWilliams and the other members of the office staff as we walked to my office. The two warriors sat down as I moved to the chair behind my desk. I wasn't sure about leaving them next to each other, but I could see they were both exhausted. I was hoping they would not explode again. They stared at each other with hate flaming in their eyes. I had to break the hateful trance they were creating.

"Ladies, this is too much for me to deal with. I don't know what to do with all this." They both looked as if they just woke up from a deep sleep. Their hair was pulled up on the sides of their heads, pointing outward. They were covered from head to toe with dirt and pine needles. They argued back and forth like fifth graders, and at one moment I thought the battle was going to explode again in the office. The reason for the argument was never quite clear and I wasn't really interested in the reasons behind the fight. I told them both they could no longer represent the school or the P.T.A. They both cried and left my office. The strangest part of the whole thing was that they drove off together in the same car. Were people crazy, or what?

Breakfast With A Parent

The next morning started with an angry father throwing a breakfast tray full of food at me while I sat at my desk. I guess if I had been on my cafeteria duty I would have been able to assist him with his complaint before he made the walk from the cafeteria to my office. With ninety-eight percent of our students being served a free breakfast, I was always ready for a dissatisfied customer, or two. It startled me when the food items from the tray flew past my head and hit the wall behind me. It was something no one would be ready for early in the morning, nor anytime, for that matter. I adjusted my eyes and saw a man standing in front of me in what I considered a defensive stance. His nostrils were flared and his empty hands were clenched fists hanging at his side. He spoke first.

"Does that look like a good breakfast to you?" I tried not to react, as I looked at my new acquaintance. My heart pounded in my chest again. I wanted to stay calm, but I knew it would be difficult with him still standing in front of me that way. It was time to respond.

"I'm not sure, sir. I didn't have a chance to see it. It went by me so fast." The irate father didn't like my response.

"Oh! You think this is funny, do ya?"

"No sir, I don't think this is funny at all.   But, you have to understand you just threw a plate of food at me, food that was given to your child free of charge. I'm not sure how to react to this. No one has thrown food at me before." I had forgotten about Janella. I should have said he was the first adult to throw food at me. " This is new to me and I'm sorry you're not getting the reaction you want."

"Well, when I used to get free breakfast at school we got good stuff to eat. Not this crap."

Now, this man was about thirty years old and after his statement about being on free breakfast it made me think that the welfare system had not worked for him. Not only was he on free breakfast as a child, but now, his child was too. He grew up expecting the system to take care of him and his children without his having to be a successful provider. How sad is that?

"Sir, I think milk, orange juice, toast with jelly and a fruit cup is a very good breakfast for anyone who may be hungry. If that's not enough for you and your child then I suggest you feed your child at home and we'll feed the child here too. You do know you don't have to eat breakfast here at all if you're unhappy with what we serve. It's your choice." The idiot was still acting crazy.

"He should have grits, eggs and real breakfast stuff like I did. I'm callin' downtown and report your stupid menu and your attitude." Why do mad parents always want to call "downtown"? Were people crazy or what?

The breakfast stains on my wall set the tone for the day. Maybe I should have taken the early encounter as a bad omen and just gone home. I tried not to think about the flying breakfast during the day as I worked with the student council putting our Thanksgiving baskets together for area families in need of holiday assistance. I checked the list of basket recipients to be sure my food-throwing friend wasn't picked for a basket. I sure didn't want free can goods thrown at me next.

The day had not started on a very positive note. I needed to find something to lift my spirits and get me in the holiday mood. I knew the best way to feel good was to visit our kindergarten classes. They were preparing for the annual Thanksgiving feast. Our kindergarten classes put on a Pilgrim and Indian dinner each year. It was a very special project and the entire school was involved. It was one of those great school events that made our efforts, as educators seem worthwhile. The dinner was one of my favorite happenings each year.

Devil Dog

I entered the kindergarten building, and I was very impressed with the student's Thanksgiving paintings I saw on the walls in the hall. There was a great feeling when you saw the creativity of a five year old. I would visit Ms. Grant's class first and then I would go to the others afterward. I had no idea the next shock of the day was waiting around the corner of the hallway. I turned the corner and there it was. I couldn't have missed it if I tried.

There was a woman lying face down on the floor of the hall. There was a pool of blood on the floor under her head and one of her wrists was bleeding. A dog chain lay on the floor next to the woman. Part of it was wrapped around her bleeding wrist. A huge, black Rottweiler stood next to her with his tongue out, licking her head. I never liked those Devil dogs ever since I saw them in the movie, "The Omen".

When the dog saw me it barked and ran to the other end of the hallway. If he had waited a second after the bark, I would have been the one running. It was hard to understand how no one had heard or seen the woman before my arrival. I guess nothing interferes with good teaching.

When the dog barked the teachers came out into the hall. I suggested they all stay in their rooms with the students as long as the dog was free in the hall. I asked Ms. Brown to call the main office and tell someone to call a rescue unit to assist me. I talked to the lady, but she didn't respond. I was really afraid she was dead. The blood was coming from her head and it looked as if she had hit her head on the floor when she fell. I thought perhaps the big dog had pulled her down because of the broken dog chain that snaked around her wrist. Several teachers came to assist me, but we could not revive the injured woman. We did find her pulse beating and she was breathing. She was still unconscious on the floor when the paramedics from the fire/rescue unit entered the hall and went to work on her injuries.

They were able to stop the bleeding from her head. I could see the cut was not very big, so I guess it is true that even small cuts on the head bleed badly. It took awhile, but the paramedics were able to bring her back to consciousness.

The moment she woke up our problems multiplied ten fold. She went wild. She fought the paramedics as if she were a man in the street. She hit, kicked and scratched at anyone near her. It took all of us to hold her and keep her from hurting any of us. The paramedics had worked so hard to get her off the floor and now we were all trying to get her back down there. It was crazy and so was she. She was handcuffed and physically carried to my office so we could get her away from the teachers and the children. The Rottweiler was tied to the bicycle rack outside at the front of the school. The woman remained handcuffed and was placed in a chair in front of my desk. The struggle was over. She sat staring straight ahead with a distant look in her eyes. I'm sure hitting her head caused part of the distant look, but there was more behind the hollow eyes of the strange lady sitting there. It was easy to see she was under the influence of drugs or alcohol. The police were called to pick her up. None of the paramedics were hurt during the physical confrontation. They were able to avoid getting hit or bitten and they were also able to keep from hurting her. The well-trained young men had done a great job and worked up quite a sweat. You always work harder when you try not to hurt someone who is trying to hurt you.

As we waited for the police to arrive she told us she was there to pick up her nephew from kindergarten. She couldn't remember how she got on the floor or anything about her injuries. She did give us her nephew's name and we were able to call his mother, Mrs. Mead. The lady was Mrs. Mead's sister and Mrs. Mead asked me to keep her at school until she could get there. The strange lady was not supposed to be picking the child up from school. I told her the police had been called and I agreed to wait for her arrival before the police took her. She lived near the school and said she was on her way. The police and Mrs. Mead arrived at the same time. Mrs. Mead walked into my office.

"I want those handcuffs off my sister." A police officer stepped into the room.

"No ma'am. We can't do that." Even though the rescue firemen had handcuffed the lady they were still bound by the police regulations about leaving the handcuffs on an arrested suspect.

"Take those things off her, right now." Mrs. Mead made her demand again.

"She's too violent and we need to protect everybody, including her." Mrs. Mead was still angry, but she sat down.

"This is my sister, Helen. She is supposed to be at my house. She has a drinking problem and I assure you if you let her go with me, this will never happen again. I'll take her to the doctor and have her injuries checked." Mrs. Mead realized the police were there to arrest her sister for the disturbance she had caused. She asked to talk to me privately, before the arrest took place. I agreed and we stepped into another office.

"My sister has serious emotional problems as you have already seen here today. She was recently released from prison. She has been gone for two years. The family is struggling to help her. I can see we are not doing such a good job. I am embarrassed and ashamed this has happened. Please allow me to take her home and I promise she will never bother you again. I am so sorry." The policeman in charge said it was up to me, that they would do whatever I wanted. I asked them to take the handcuffs off of Helen and I let her go home with her sister. Was I crazy, or what? Were people crazy, or what?

At midnight that same night, I was called by the county school security about the fire alarm sounding at the school. They requested that I go to school and take care of the problem. I knew the loud alarm was a real disturbance to the families living near the school, so I hurried to get there. I always took my gun with me whenever I had to go back to the school late at night.

When I arrived, the alarm bell was still blasting loudly. I felt bad for our good neighbors. I turned off the alarm and reset the box, but I could not find the reason that caused the alarm to go off. The school was quiet and secure. I got into my car and drove back out through the gate I had opened when I arrived. I stopped and got out of the car to lock the gate behind me. There was someone standing across the street in the dark. It scared me and I reached into the car for my gun I had put on the passenger seat.

It was Helen, the strange lady I had dealt with earlier that day. She stepped in front of my car as if she could stop me from leaving by standing in the way and blocking my exit.

"You're the ass-hole that was gonna have me arrested today." She stepped toward the side of my car where I was standing. I could see the shock on her face when I pointed the gun at her nose.

"If you take another step I'll shoot you." She was frozen stiff with fear in front of me and I think she instantly sobered up. She was really scared and she didn't know what to do. Even with the gun in my hand my heart raced in my chest or perhaps it was because of the gun. She said nothing as I sat down in the driver's seat of my car. I continued pointing the gun at her out of the car window as I drove past her and out the entrance of the school. I saw a policeman in a patrol car in the parking lot of a local tavern as I left the area. I stopped and told him about the lady and the earlier incident. He told me he would go back to the school and see if she was still there. I went home.

Thanksgiving Head Lice 101

When Ms. Sibble walked into my office one morning I asked myself two questions: "Why do I have to have all the parents who smell so bad and was there no soap in this part of town at all?" We were meeting because three of her children had head lice and I had removed them from school until they were treated. We had even supplied her with the medicated shampoo so she could treat the entire family. I was supposed to explain to Ms. Sibble about cleaning the house, washing the bed linens and the furniture to get rid of all the creatures and the eggs that would hatch later. This was another part of my job as a principal that was not covered in the educational college courses. There was no "Head Lice Detection and Treatment 101" at any university. I explained it would not do any good to merely wash the children's hair and then let the lice from the house infect them again. My intentions were to talk about the problem and get some cooperation with the head lice situation, but Ms. Sibble had another motive for her visit.

She pushed a filthy, rusty baby stroller into my office when she came in. I assumed there was a baby under the dirty blue blanket that covered the seat part of the stroller. Not once did I have any desire to look under that nasty blanket. I had seen the movie "Rosemary's

Baby" and nothing could have made me look under that blanket. She had also brought another child with her. He looked to be about three years old. He sat next to her in one of the office chairs. The boy's nose was running like an open faucet and it was easy to see he had wiped his dripping nose on his shirtsleeve more than once or twice. I had heard from other parents that Ms. Sibble's ninth grade daughter had given birth recently, so I assumed the baby under the dirty blue blanket was the new arrival. I also assumed there was actually a baby under the blanket, but I really hadn't heard one or seen one up to that point in the visit. I did see the welfare dollar signs light up in Ms. Sibble's blood shot eyes. She was a master at working the welfare system and using it to her advantage. She considered it her job to get all she could from whom ever she could with any and all means at her disposal. I didn't like her at all. I hated the fact she was in the welfare system. She received food stamps, her children were on free breakfast and free lunch and yet when you called her house she had an answering machine and call waiting. Something was wrong with that picture to me. She was like the man who threw the breakfast at me, always taking. It was a way of life and they had mastered it.

I had no idea I was about to get a lesson from Ms. Sibble, but I did leave myself wide open and I deserved it. Before I could share all my head lice expertise, she took over the conversation.

"Mr. Reynolds, I'm so upset with you and the school." I really didn't care that she was upset and I actually couldn't believe she said that to me. I thought she was blaming the school for her head lice problems. Parents always blame the school when their children have head lice.

"Ms. Sibble, this head lice thing is awful. Your children cannot go on infecting the entire school. We should be upset with you." We were not on the same wavelength at all.

"Oh, I'm not talkin'bout them damn bugs. I'm talkin'bout the Thanksgivin' baskets ya'll give out yesterday. We needed one bad. I just knew we was gonna get one as a needy family in the school. I was really countin' on that basket. We don't have nothin' now. We got a basket last year and the year before. What happened?"

I didn't have much of an answer for her because I didn't know the answer. A number of clubs at school had bought ten turkeys and filled two large baskets with over one hundred different canned goods in each individual basket to be given to ten needy families in the area. They were great baskets. I had nothing to do with the selection of the families receiving the baskets. I only knew everyone was talking about how wonderful the baskets were and how pleased the families were as well. I explained my thoughts to Ms. Sibble and I told her I was sorry she was overlooked that year. Of course, she was not finished with me. She was an expert.

"Ya'll don't have nothin' left?" She was pitiful and it was obvious she had been pitiful many times before. She was a master at being pitiful too. I told her I would see what I could do, but I couldn't promise her anything. We didn't say much about the head lice problem. I did tell her we were going to check her children each morning before they could go to class and if they still had the head lice they would be sent home. She didn't like my tone and she wanted our meeting to end. She left the office, but her odor lingered. Jerome, our custodian, saved me with his little magic spray bottle filled with a pleasant smelling disinfectant.

I couldn't get the thought about the Sibble children not having anything for Thanksgiving dinner out of my mind. I just couldn't help it. I knew that was what she wanted, but I still felt bad for the children. If I did help it would be for the children, not her. Before the day ended, I met with our student council and asked them to try and collect as many can goods as they could for the next day. They agreed to help and we would try to create one more basket for the Sibble family. We didn't have any more money so I decided that I would buy the Thanksgiving bird.

As usual, the students came through the next morning with seventy different can goods and they fixed up a nicely decorated holiday basket.

I went to the store for the turkey. When I arrived at the store I only had a ten-dollar bill with me, so I bought a large baking hen for the basket. It was a nice bird and it took the entire ten dollars. When I returned to school I called Ms. Sibble and told her to "come and get it". I was proud of our students and their unselfish efforts. Ms. Sibble said she would be there as soon as she found her brother. He had a truck and would give her a ride to the school. Within thirty minutes an old rusty green truck drove up to the front of the school.

Ms. Sibble and who I assumed was her brother, came into the front office. I met them at the counter. I didn't want him or her in my office and I didn't want a conversation with them at all. I pointed out the basket and a box with some extra can goods. Ms. Sibble grabbed the basket and her brother grabbed the box. I followed them with the hen in a bag. The man said nothing as he put the box in the back of his truck and jumped into the driver's seat. I didn't like him either. Ms. Sibble put the basket next to the box and whispered to me.

"I'll have to share it with him, he don't do nothin' for nothin'." I really didn't like anything about her or her brother. I just wanted them gone so I handed her the bag. She grabbed it and quickly looked inside. I couldn't believe my ears. I thought I was having a serious daydream. She yelled to her brother.

"Harland, it's just an ol' bakin' hen. It ain't even a turkey." She closed the bag and with a disgusted look on her ugly face, walked to the passenger's side of the truck. I was speechless, she wasn't. She looked back at me. " Who the hell wants a bakin' hen for Thanksgivin'. It ain't Thanksgivin' without a turkey."

I wanted to beat her to death, personally, with the frozen hen. I lost all my holiday spirit. I visualized myself hitting her with the bird. I wanted to pull all the can goods from the back of the truck. I wanted to beat Harland with the chicken too and I had never seen him before. I don't remember her getting into the truck, but the truck moved away, baking hen and all. Were people crazy or what?

The holiday week continued, as we sent fifty-three of our students home with head lice, an epidemic of biblical proportion by any standard. The school supplied the medicated shampoo and we even treated many of the children in the clinic bathroom at school where we had a bathtub and shower installed for our students. It was educationally sound for us to treat the students for head lice at school so they would not stay home and miss school time. Plus, we could be sure the treatment was done properly. We were breaking county policy, however, and there was a problem of liability. The practice of washing heads at school had to stop. The head lice epidemic was our holiday gift from the Sibble family. Or perhaps, it was some perverse curse brought down on the entire school as a punishment for me buying a baking hen and not a turkey.

Aunt Pat

Once again I found myself waiting for Friday to arrive as if it was the magical day that would make the days that came before it go away. The more I thought about it, the more I realized the bad days actually did go away by Friday so why did I allow them to stay with me? Why do we wish our lives away waiting for some other day to arrive? I was hoping to get away from school early that afternoon so I could meet my wife and daughter at my son's soccer game. Our bookkeeper, Ms. Gilmer, interrupted a vision I was having of my son scoring the winning goal.

"Mr. Reynolds, one of the kindergarten students is still waiting for someone to pick him up." I turned to see a handsome, dark haired, dark eyed, five-year-old boy. He looked to be of Italian or perhaps Arabic decent. "His name is Gabriel and he's been waiting since 1:30. The home phone has been disconnected and there is no answer at the emergency number." I really wanted to go home, but little Gabriel needed to go home too.

"Gabriel, if Mr. Reynolds gives you a ride can you show me where you live?" He smiled and nodded his head. I had an idea where he lived. I wrote down the address just in case I had to go "in search of." Acme Street was about six blocks away from the school and I was sure the child was smart enough to direct me to his house if we got close enough to it. Our conversation during the ride was most interesting. He was adorable as he started the conversation.

"I live in a junky blue house. It's ugly. I can't go in if Aunt Pat's home. I can't be alone in the house with Aunt Pat. Uncle David has to be there or I can't go in." Now was my curiosity awakened, or what?

"Why can't you stay with Aunt Pat?"

" 'Cause she does crazy stuff to people. She's on crack. Crack makes you do crazy stuff. I can't stay with her." We turned onto Acme Street. Gabriel was excited.

"There's my house, the blue one. Ain't it ugly?" Gabriel was right; it was ugly, real ugly. It was like a junkyard, complete with three junkyard dogs sleeping in the dirt. There was trash all over and two cars sitting up on concrete blocks covered most of the grassless yard. The front door of the house was open and there was loud music playing. I stopped the car, but Gabriel did not make a move to get out. It was easy to see he was concerned about who might be in the house. I didn't like it at all. We both shared the same concerns and we sat there for a few seconds staring at the opened front door. To my surprise, Gabriel broke our moment of silence.

"If Aunt Pat's here, I'll have to go back to school with you until Uncle David comes to get me." Gabriel was really afraid and I could feel his discomfort. He was too handsome and too little to have such worries and fears in his life. I wanted to go home too, but Gabriel had become my responsibility. I was the principal.

"I'll see who's here." I wasn't pleased with the possibility of meeting Aunt Pat, especially when she wasn't expecting visitors, but I had to do something. That good old warning system of mine started pounding in my chest as I walked toward the opened front door. I was almost at the doorway when Gabriel joined me.

Even though he was only five years old I was more than happy to have his company and support at that moment. I liked Gabriel. We walked to the front door and I knocked on the door facing. Gabriel stood behind me as I stepped up into the opened doorway.

There was no furniture in the front room except for a small table with a radio on it. There was a man on the floor near the door, who appeared to be sleeping. Gabriel whispered to me.

"That's Uncle David." There was another body on the floor across the empty room in the far corner. It was a woman with long blonde hair. She was curled up with her back to me. She was completely naked. Gabriel saw her too and whispered to me again.

"That's Aunt Pat." I wasn't surprised at his identification of the body, but I was very uncomfortable about standing in that room. Then Gabriel stole my heart again. He picked up a dirty wrinkled shirt off the floor and covered his Aunt Pat the best he could. I couldn't believe that little boy, with all his obvious problems, had such compassion and understanding. It was easy to fall in love with Gabriel. He was a class act living in the bowels of life.

I turned my attention to Uncle David as Gabriel bent down and shook his uncle's shoulder. Uncle David came off the floor as if someone had set him on fire. It scared us both. Uncle David added to our fear.

"Who the hell are you? Get out of my house!" Uncle David didn't see Gabriel when he erupted from his coma. He stepped toward me and I thought I was going to have to either run or defend myself. I didn't want to do either, but I would have chosen running first. I had been extremely stupid and I should have never entered that house. It was a bad situation and I realized I was actually an intruder in a strange house. I stood there eye-to-eye with Uncle David while Aunt Pat lay naked on the floor. Uncle David could have killed me on the spot and probably would have gotten away with it. My instinct to run was very heavy at that moment, but then Uncle David focused in on Gabriel.

"Gabe, where'd you come from?" Uncle David stopped and tried to clear his head. I tried to use his head clearing moment to my advantage.

"I'm Mr. Reynolds, the principal from Gabriel's school. You didn't pick him up today. School's over." Uncle David looked at Gabriel, but he talked to me.

"Oh Man, I'm sorry. I work at night. What time is it?" I looked at my watch.

"It's almost five o'clock. He's been out of school since one thirty."

"I fell asleep. I'm really sorry, man." Uncle David saw Aunt Pat on the floor across the room. "Pat, get up and get some clothes on." Aunt Pat didn't move. Uncle David looked at me. "She's all screwed up, man. You know, that crack shit. I try to keep her away from it, but she gets it while I'm at work." I hadn't realized Gabriel was holding my hand. I guess he grabbed it when Uncle David jumped up and scared us. Loving Gabriel was easy.

I couldn't wait to see my son play soccer that night and spend time with my family. I wanted to hug and kiss both my children. I wanted to hug Gabriel, too.

I later gave the information about what I had seen at Gabriel's house to Mrs. McWilliams. We watched Gabriel closely when he was at school. I don't think I ever saw Aunt Pat again, but I'm not sure I would have recognized her if I saw her from the front and fully clothed. I did have to deal with Uncle David a few times because of Gabriel's poor attendance. After Mrs. McWilliams arranged a visit to Gabriel's house by a representative from the HRS, Uncle David, Aunt Pat and Gabriel moved away. People like that are always on the move or on the run, especially when the rent comes due. It has been said that as educators we cannot save all the children who pass through our lives. You always want that adage to not be true, but it is.

Citizen's Arrest

The school was buzzing that Monday morning about the wild events that happened in the neighborhood over the weekend. The police had raided four different houses that were in the neighborhood around the school and large amounts of the 60's drug, LSD, had been confiscated. A former student, now a teenager, had been shot and killed Saturday night. He was standing at the corner of the campus property where the school safety patrol stood in the afternoon each day. Our cafeteria manager had died suddenly of a heart attack. It was a sad, but typical Monday morning. Wasn't that scary?

It was the third time in as many weeks we had heard the same rumors. There was supposed to be a blue van driving around the area near the school. It would stop and the driver would ask little girls if they wanted a ride to school. The police had been notified and we were all on the lookout for the neighborhood intruder. Three of our students were supposedly able to identify the van and the driver.

There was also talk of another problem near the school where a man was running out of the woods near a small bridge and exposing himself to the students as they walked to school early in the morning. A large number of students had seen the flasher and the parents were up in arms about the two perverts roaming the streets of Sin City.

I was sitting at my desk writing a letter to the parents concerning the information we had about the intruders. The letter also provided a few safety tips. Schools always have safety tips. I stopped writing and looked out the window of my office. I was trying to find the proper words for the delicate subject matter. Suddenly two grown, white men riding bicycles went flying past the window. The speed of the bikes told me something was very wrong. I left my office to find out where they were going in such a hurry. I hoped they were just passing through, but for some reason, I knew they were not. I stepped outside the building to meet them, but I only saw the back wheel on one of the bikes as it turned the corner at the edge of the building. They were moving toward the middle of the central courtyard on the school campus. At their speed, it would be impossible for me to overtake them at any destination on the school grounds. I took the shortest route through the main building in an attempt to locate the intruders. "Call the police. Tell them we have adult intruders at the school", was my request to Mrs. Highsmith as I took the shortcut through the main office.

When I finally made it to the courtyard, my heartbeat stepped up a notch when I saw both bicycles lying on the ground outside a third grade classroom. I heard voices, but I could not understand what was being said. I entered the classroom and saw one of the men standing over a black child who was sitting in a desk. The man was angry and yelling at the scared child. The other man stood near the teacher and was actually standing in her way by her desk. It was easy for me to see the fear on Ms. Whiteard's face. No teacher is prepared for angry adult intruders taking over the classroom. The entire class was afraid. The angry man was eye-to-eye with the little third grader. I took a deep breath and did my job.

"Leave that child alone!" That was the best I could do. Like everyone else, I was scared too. Both men turned and looked at me as my heart pounded in my chest and my mouth went dry. Fear does that. "You can't be here and scare these children like this. Please leave.

We've called the police." They turned all of their attention to me then and I knew that was good for the teacher and the students, but not for me.

Both men moved in my direction and I noticed wicked, half smiles on their faces. That made me even more afraid. It was as if they had come to hurt somebody and it didn't matter to them who it was going to be. As they moved, I backed out of the classroom. Our assistant principal, Mr. Marayag, an ex-Navy man of Philippine descent, came to assist me on the sidewalk. I was glad to see a friendly face. He wanted to make a stand with me and it was obvious Mr. Marayag would have fought to protect me. I appreciated his courage and have never forgotten it to this day, but I didn't want to add to the confrontation. I was hoping for a better way out of the situation. Mr. Marayag was in a defensive stance and prepared to do battle with the two intruders if it came to such an action. He reminded me of Mr. Miyagi in the movie, "The Karate Kid". I liked Mr. Marayag. I got his attention.

"Go make sure the police are coming." Mr. Marayag didn't want to leave me. It was obvious he was not afraid and he would fight if necessary. He took the responsibility of making sure the police would find us when they arrived. The two good old boys heard my request as they both stepped closer to me on the sidewalk. The bigger of the two men spoke first.

"You don't have time for the police, mister. We're gonna beat your ass and then that little nigger's ass too, long before those pigs will answer a call out here. You're getting' ready to get your coat dirty." They both laughed and moved toward me again. They were happy intruders, but I saw nothing funny about the situation at all. At that moment I'm sure I had some type of mental lapse from the pressure and the stress I was facing. I actually thought I heard that music from the Clint Eastwood movie, "Good, Bad and the Ugly" and I found myself taking off my coat. Mr. Marayag's courage had inspired me and I wasn't sure what to do next, but like Clint, I was standing alone. I found the words.

"You must know I can't allow you to come here and hurt a child, or anyone else for that matter." I wanted to remind them I was the principal, but I didn't think it was the right time so I didn't mention that. For some reason they were no longer moving toward me so I took the moment to talk some more.

"As mad as you two seem to be I'd like to run away, but what kind of man would do that? You know I can't do that." I stood there trying to keep my legs from shaking and hoping the police would hurry to my rescue. They always save people in those situations like me in the movies, so where were they? I was getting very close to getting what is called a "first class butt whippin'" and I was doing everything I could to hide my fear. Dogs can always sense fear and take advantage of that weakness. I was facing two real dogs and they were more than ready to double team me and take advantage of my weaknesses.

Then I knew I had done my job when I heard all the doors to the classrooms near me being closed and locked by the teachers. All the students were safe. I was the only one left to save and I couldn't see that happening any time soon. I had also decided if the big, bad and ugly continued their hostile action toward me, I could run into the large courtyard. As frightened as I was, I knew they would have a hard time catching me if I chose to take flight. My confidence level increased when I noticed they were both wearing cowboy boots; big cowboy boots. It made me feel better about out running them both. It wasn't the bravest plan, but it was a plan. For some reason I took my coat off and placed it on a small bush next to the sidewalk. I guess I was planning to run, but they thought I was making a stand. The second and smaller man broke the silence and spoke for the first time.

"This guy's nuts, Walter. He don't care if we do kick his ass. He's crazy." Walter nodded his head in agreement. Then he began to question me as if I was the problem.

"What the hell's wrong with you? What kinda teacher are you, anyway? Do you work here?" I wanted to keep the talk going.

"What's wrong with me? What's wrong with you? You're the ones who've come here to hurt a third grader."

"That little nigger pushed my boy in the ditch and he got eight stitches in his foot. Somebody's gonna pay for that." I was more than willing to add to our conversation.

"You can't bring these problems to school like this. Now, if you two will come to my office I will try to help you. I'm Mr. Reynolds, the principal." Like an excited child the second man joined in.

"The principal? Damn Walter, he's the principal!" I wanted to laugh at his strange reaction to my identity, but I didn't want to press my luck.

"I can't talk to you under these conditions. If you want to talk, it will have to be in my office or you will have to leave the school." I wasn't sure I should have said that, but it was said and I couldn't take it back. I waited for Walter's reaction, as I remained in my sprint mode, ready to haul butt at any indication of bodily harm headed in my direction.

I was surprised and cautious when both men picked up their bikes and walked with me toward my office. I've known people who made the mistake of relaxing during confrontational situations and they got hurt when they didn't expect it. I was not going to be sucker punched by either of the intruders so I walked at a safe and ready to run if need be, distance from the two good old boys. My feet were on "ready".

The three of us passed Mr. Marayag at the door of the main office. He was still in his protective state and he gave both men a serious look to let them know he was still around and ready to rumble. Again, I appreciated his courage. I could tell the office staff was as surprised as I was that we had actually made it to the office. I'm sure they thought I was crazy for bringing them there, but I didn't really think they would come with me. Both men were strange and almost like children, especially the second and smaller man. They sat down in front of my desk. The smaller man couldn't help himself.

"Damn Walter, I ain't been to this office in years. I used to go here. You got a paddle?" It was so nice having one of our returning alumni sitting in my office. Walter was a little more crass than his companion.

"Would you shut the hell up? You sound like an idiot." The smaller man stopped talking and it was easy to see he was mad at Walter. In his quiet state it was obvious he was scanning the room for that paddle he was so interested in. He was probably trying to see if it was the same one that had been used on him years ago. Walter noticed his friend's visual search too, but he didn't say anything about it. I'm not sure why, but I held up my candy jar.

"Can I sweeten you gentlemen up with some candy?" They both smiled at my attempt to ease the tension. I couldn't believe it when Walter reached into the opened jar and took out a piece of candy. His friend took out two mints and one butterscotch. Only a few minutes before those two desperados were going to beat my brains out and now we were sharing star-lite mints. Are people crazy or what?

They were the Spearing brothers, Walter and Ben. Walter's son had been hurt and they were upset with the number of blacks attending the school and living in the neighborhood.

"We ain't prejudice or nothin', we just don't want 'em in the neighborhood," was Walter's rationale. He attempted his own light moment when he said the candy must have done the trick. He was sorry he had gone after the little third grade boy. He really wasn't going to hurt him; he just wanted to scare him a little. I wanted to tell Walter that scaring the child was just as bad, but he was trying to apologize in his own way so I left it at that. He said his son, Walter Jr., would have to take care of the problem himself or keep getting pushed into the ditch. They both shook my hand and left. I hoped it was the last time I would ever deal with the Spearing brothers, but sadly enough that would not be the case. The police never came that day. The very next morning I took a phone call I wish I had not answered, but I was the principal.

"Good morning. This is Bill Reynolds, may I help you?"

"Reynolds?"

"Yes, this is Bill Reynolds."

"This is Walter Spearing. You know, the one who was gonna kick your ass yesterday." I had better greetings in the morning, but I knew right away who was talking.

"Yes, Mr. Spearing, I recognize your voice."

"Well, the queer's in the woods down by the bridge and he's already showed his dick to some of the little girls this mornin'. Let's go down there and kick his ass." I was shocked by his request.

"Mr. Spearing, I can't go with you and do something like that. What would people think of a school principal who did such a thing?"

"Ben said to call you and you would probably go with us for the kids. We'll come get ya. You could make it official when we catch the nasty bastard."

"Please don't come here to get me. I can't go with you."

"Then what should we do with the queer?"

"I'll call the police and send them down there. You try to find out where he's hiding. Then, when the police come you can show them." Now, instead of leaving those instructions and hanging up the phone, I had to add another thought and another mistake on my part. "If you see him and can get to him, make a citizen's arrest and I'll make sure the police will be there soon." Walter hung up first without another word. It seemed the thought of a citizen's arrest overshadowed his desire to be congenial. I called the police and told them about the flasher at the bridge. Within an hour after Walter's phone call, a young police officer stood at the counter in our main office.

"I'm looking for Mr. Reynolds."

"I'm Bill Reynolds.' The young officer was strictly business.

"Mr. Reynolds, please don't tell these folks around here to make a citizen's arrest. A Mr. Spearing told us you suggested they capture the flasher and you would send us to get him."

"I did tell him that. I thought you would be down there before they actually caught him."

"Not quite, sir. When we got there, they had already caught a man, beat the hell out of him and then tied him to a post on Mr. Spearing's front porch. When they caught him he must have had his pants down so they would not let him pull them back up. They wanted him to stay exposed until we arrived as proof he was the flasher. They also had a group of young children from the neighborhood, mostly little girls, in a line walking past the man so they could identify the evidence hanging down. They have violated all the man's rights. We untied him. We offered to take him to the hospital, but he just wanted to get away. He probably is the flasher. I don't think he'll be back, but we had to let him go. He could press charges against Mr. Spearing, but I don't think he will."

I was speechless and very sorry I had caused such trouble. I was glad, however, the flasher was gone. It really didn't matter what method was used to convince him to leave.

Later that day, I had another policeman visit my office. He wanted to talk to one of our fourth grade girls. Her parents had reported she had been approached by a man in the blue van and she would be able to recognize him if she saw him again. The police officer wanted the girl to look at some pictures of known sex offenders in the area and perhaps she would be able to pick him out.

I called Jenny to my office and remained with her while the officer explained what he wanted her to do. When he handed her the first picture her eyes popped open and she almost jumped out of the chair.

"That's him! That's him! He was the man in the blue van."

I couldn't believe it. The first picture she saw was the culprit. She was so positive. I was as excited as she was. The officer took the picture from her hand and handed it to me.

"Have you seen this man around here?" I took the picture. It was Walter Spearing.

It's Hot Outside

During that same week a number of students who were walking home began littering the sidewalks. They threw rocks at dogs and they even destroyed a number of mailboxes along the sidewalk. Some of the residents had taken matters into their own hands and had begun confronting the students. Many innocent children were chased and frightened by the dogs when some of the locals let their dogs loose from chains and fences in order to discourage the students from walking near their houses. A number of our "fine" neighbors even used water hoses and squirted the children as they walked home. I decided to walk with that particular group of students until things calmed down. My presence seemed to end the battle.

We also had a new student enter the school that week. John was from Idaho and he was staying at the local Boy's Home until his grandfather could be located. John had been a witness to his father's death at the hands of his real mother and her boyfriend. Not only did John see the actual killing, he also rode in the car when they took his father's body into the woods and buried it. John was in the back seat of the car and his father's dead body was in the trunk. Both his mother and the boyfriend had been committed to prison for the crime. It would be an extreme understatement to say John had emotional problems. He was awful in school. How could a child experience such mental anguish? He was with us for about ten days and in that amount of time, he assaulted students and teachers and he attacked workers at the Boy's Home. It wasn't his fault, but I was still glad when he was gone.

Many times, students bring serious problems with them to school. These are usually secrets and unknown to teachers, who hopes the child will be basically normal and able to learn. Teachers need to know about the students, but that is not always the case.

Frankie and Wayne were perfect examples of children coming to school with too much to deal with on the outside. We struggled with the two boys and their mother until the mother exploded one day in my office. The frustration of the children's problems at school caused her to tell me this story.

"How would you act if you came home one day and found your father's brains dripping from the ceiling of your trailer where he had put a shotgun in his mouth and pulled the trigger?" I worked harder to help the two boys. We all did.

I was just recovering from the Spearing brother intruder incident when I saw another strange man run into the office. He looked to be in his twenties, he wore only a pair of shorts, no shirt or shoes and he was sweating profusely. At first I thought he needed help. He had the look of someone in an emergency situation. The wild look on his face scared me. My fear increased when he ran into our clinic area and into the bathroom where he closed and locked the door. I moved to the clinic and stopped at the closed door. I listened at the door and could hear the water running in the bathtub. One of our teachers, Ms. Shepard was in the clinic helping a student when the man entered the bathroom. Good teachers always seem to know what to do. Ms. Shepard moved past me with the student.

"I'll call the police, Mr. Reynolds. Be careful, please." I nodded and knocked on the door.

"Excuse me young man. Are you okay in there?" He did not respond. The water was still running. "If you're hurt we can help you.

Are you hurt?   Did you just have to use our bathroom?   Please say something to me, or I will have to call the police.   You can't act like this in our school.   I need to know your problem."   The office staff had moved to the door of the clinic to be with me.   I motioned to them to stay out of the clinic.   I didn't know when he was going to come out of his hiding place, or what he would do to get away.   The longer the stand off went on the more frightened I became.   Then, I heard the most wonderful voice.   It was our bookkeeper, Ms. Gilmer.

"Mr. Reynolds, the police are here."   They must have been near the school when they got the call, because they had never answered a call that fast.   I explained what had occurred and alerted them to the fact he was still in the bathroom.   The two young police officers went through the same ritual I had done moments before.   The only difference was that they identified themselves as police officers.   Again, he did not respond.

The door could only be locked and unlocked from the inside, a problem I had already reported to our maintenance department.   I should have had it fixed sooner.   The water stopped running and we all stood there waiting for the young man to come out.   He didn't.   The young police officers were impatient and one went to his car for a tool kit.   In a matter of moments the two officers were removing the hinge pins of the door.   When the last pin was removed one policeman pulled the door as the other drew his gun and held it up, aiming it at who ever was in the small room.

The intruder was completely naked and he was sitting in the bathtub full of water.   The policeman with the gun moved into the small room.

"Don't move mister!   Put your hands in the air and don't stand up until I tell you to."   The young man in the tub lifted his hands above his head.   The second officer moved into the room and pulled the young man from the tub, turning him toward the wall and placing handcuffs on the wrists.   The policeman with the gun recited the man's rights as the other moved the naked man into the clinic.   There was a sheet on one of the beds in the clinic and I handed it to one of the officers to cover the intruder. He was dripping water all over the carpet as he was moved along. The young man finally spoke as the two officers moved him out of the room and toward the police car. He looked at Ms. Gilmer standing at the front counter.

"Damn, it's hot outside, ain't it?"

Adult Eyes

When I first saw Sally, I was taken by her sad adult looking eyes. She was quiet and withdrawn and had what I call an "empty look". Her eyes did not fit her child features. Her eyes seemed older and looked as if they were part of the wrong face. Later, I asked Mrs. McWilliams about Sally's eyes and she told me it could be a sign of an abused child. The reason for Sally's visit to my office was so I could see a number of marks on her arms, legs and back. Mrs. McWilliams was concerned with the child's safety at home. Sally told me her mother had beaten her because she had broken a glass while washing dishes two days ago. I had to get my thoughts together as to what to do next.

Mrs. McWilliams informed me that Sally wore long dresses with long sleeves, and also sweaters, even when the weather was warm. Abused children often wear certain clothes to hide bruises or marks on their bodies. The marks were found when Sally's classroom teacher, Ms. Keller, talked Sally into taking her sweater off in the classroom because it was very hot. Even though Sally was only eight years old, I had a feeling she had lived a lifetime already. I then made a huge mistake with regard to Sally. Instead of calling the abuse registry, I called Sally's mother and told her I needed to talk to her about Sally. I requested the meeting and Sally's mother was on her way to school. I had not met Mrs. Dalton before that day. It was a meeting I would never forget as my life continued. Mrs. McWilliams took Sally to her office while I waited for her mother. It wasn't long before the awful woman stormed into my office.

"What the hell you doin' with my child?"

I couldn't believe my eyes. Was I looking at a him, or a her? If it was Sally's mother, I was no doubt, looking at the ugliest and dirtiest woman on the earth. Only the devil could have smelled like that. I thought perhaps she had road kill in her pocket. It was awful. She was loud, aggressive and her evil look was scary and intimidating. We were all uneasy with her presence in the office. I wanted to take a deep breath to gain my composure, but I knew it would make me sick if I did. Again, I couldn't believe my eyes or my nose. If trolls really existed, the creature standing in front of me would have been the queen of the goat eaters.

"I want my child, now!" Her wild glare made my heart pound as usual and I hoped she wouldn't hear it beating. I wanted to leave, but it was my job to stay. I was the principal.

"If you continue to talk to me in this manner I will have you arrested for disturbing the educational process of the school." She moved toward me after my statement. I actually thought I was going to have to defend myself against the devil woman. It was something I had not considered until that moment. I stood up and she stopped her forward motion. She continued to amaze me.

"I don't beat Sally unless she needs it. I died once and was with Jesus for fourteen hours and He told me what to do with my life. Sally ain't none of your business and you'll find out this neighborhood won't let you mess in our business. We already got rid of three principals before you. You can be number four."

It had been said that I was the ninth principal in eleven years at the school. Perhaps the devil woman had a hand in a few of them leaving. I know I wanted to leave at that very moment.

As her aggressive attitude continued, I realized there would be no reasoning with her at all, so I asked my secretary to call the police. The wild one kicked over a chair, called me a bastard and stuck a stained, nasty finger up in my face. The amount of filthy grime and grease under her fingernails was incredible. She was either a car mechanic or she scratched dirt for a living. She roared out of the office yelling obscenities at anyone she saw. With the police on the way, I asked Mrs. McWilliams to call the abuse registry. It was something I should have done in the first place. The police arrived and after hearing about Sally's mother and seeing the marks caused by her on the child, they went to visit Sally's mother, Mrs. Dalton.

An HRS worker arrived just before school was to be dismissed and talked to Sally. She took Sally home and was going to talk to her mother. Sally did not come to school the next day. The police did not contact us and I received no phone call from the HRS representative. Mrs. McWilliams was concerned with the lack of communication. She called the HRS worker to inform her Sally had not returned to school.

Mrs. McWilliams was told Mrs. Dalton admitted she hit Sally too hard and she was very sorry she hurt her and left such marks. It would not happen again and Sally was left with her mother at home. I was also informed Sally's father drove a school bus for our county and he transported handicapped children to various schools in the area. He had been working in that capacity for twenty years. And if that news wasn't distressing enough, I was also told a number of the students he transported were being kept at the Dalton house each day after school.

The Daltons ran a daycare for the handicapped children and took care of the children until their parents got off work. I couldn't help wondering what kind of parents would leave their children in Mrs. Dalton's dirty hands. I told the HRS worker I was worried about Sally not returning to school. At my urging, the HRS worker called Mrs. Dalton to inquire as to why Sally was not in school. She was told Sally was upset about the situation at school so she let Sally stay home.

Sally would be back on Monday. I didn't like it, but I could do nothing.

On Monday morning I called Sally to my office after the pledge to the flag. When she walked into my office I noticed right away her long sleeves and collar buttoned up to the neck. She never smiled and once again, her eyes took me. I wanted to talk to her and make sure she was safe. I wondered if she had suffered any more abuse during the three days that had passed.

"Sit down, Sally. How are you this morning?"

"Fine." Her voice was very low and she kept her head down.

"Are you feeling better, now?" She nodded her head and I could see information was not going to flow from her at all. She was very nervous as she sat with me and I didn't want her to be afraid or uncomfortable in any way. I felt bad about making an eight-year-old child uneasy at school. She had enough problems without me adding to them. I tried one more time. I used school talk.

"Sally, you are a very good student. What is your best subject in school? What do you like to do best?" She looked around the room, as if she was afraid we were being watched. She then motioned to me with her index finger to come closer. It was the friendliest finger I had seen in sometime. With those adult eyes, she broke my heart as she whispered.

"Please don't make me talk to you." She leaned back in the chair. My broken heart was still able to beat, because I could hear it. I would not press her anymore, but I hated her mother.

"You can go back to class now Sally. Thank you for being so nice." I wanted to face the evil troll again.

A Piece Of Bull

Marcus had been in my office for the fifth time so far that week. Five times in three days was just too much for any student, much less a first grader. He was disrespectful to adults, fought with his teacher and his classmates, refused to do any work and used the dreaded "F" word on a regular basis. He had already been referred to the guidance counselor to be tested for emotional problems. When dealing with the younger and new students we tried to work on the behavior problems at the school without involving the parents at first. Many times, the child needed to adjust to the new situation and it might take time. Children usually reacted to our methods and the problems ended. In the case with Marcus, it was time to get his mother involved. We needed her written permission to test him for possible exceptional education placement and we also needed her help with the aggressive attitude of the first grader.

Marcus and his brother, Robert, were bus riders and came from the north side of town. It was very difficult to get many parents to visit the school from such a distance. The family had no phone so I gave Robert a letter telling their mother Marcus could not return to school until she met with me and we worked together to stop his improper behavior. Perhaps she would be the answer to the situation.

The next day Marcus, Robert and their mother rode the school bus to school from the north side of town. I was surprised, but pleased with such a fast response to my letter. Marcus and his mother, Ms. Haley, walked into my office. After our normal introduction, I began telling Ms. Haley about the attitude and antics of her son Marcus at school. As I talked, Marcus was rude, as usual, and interrupted me. I was surprised that with his mother there, he would still be so aggressive and bold.

"He's lyin' on me. People always lie on me." Her eyes widened.

"Shut your mouth. Bull. If you say another word I will knock that head of yours off your shoulders." She looked back at me. "We call him Bull at home."

Bull was mad, but didn't say anything else, as we continued. Ms. Haley listened to me and didn't say a word until I finished.

"Did you use the board on him?"

"No ma'am, I didn't. I try not to paddle any of the students, especially the young ones. Sometimes I do use the paddle on the older students at the parent's request, but I really don't like to do it. I'll leave that up to you." She gave Bull a wide-eyed look. She kept her eyes on Bull as she talked to me.

"You gotta let Bull know you don't play. He knows I don't play."

"I will allow a parent to use my paddle here in the office. Sometimes that's all it takes, but I only allow that one time. If it doesn't take care of the problem we go to other methods."

"I can't let Bull get away with this at school. I send him here to learn. He knows I don't play." She took Bull's face in her hand and squeezed his checks together. "I'm givin' this man my permission to use that board on you anytime he thinks you need it. If I have to come out to this school again, I will tear the hide off you. Do you understand me, boy?" Bull nodded his head the best he could, with her holding his face.

"I can't hear your head move."

"Yes, ma'am." She released her hold on his face.

"Mr. Reynolds, I'm gonna fire his little bad butt up and then he's gonna tell you and his teacher how sorry he is and that he is going to change. Can I use your paddle?" At that point I made another administrative mistake and handed her the wooden board. Ms. Haley took the paddle from me.

She stood Bull up and turned him around, hitting him as he turned. He made no sound and his facial expression did not change. She talked as she hit him the second time.

"If I have to come here again…" She hit him the third time. Up to that point, all three licks had been on his little butt. They were hard licks and I thought the punishment was over. It wasn't. It was just beginning. Bull still made no sound, nor flinched as if he was in pain. There was no doubt in my mind Marcus had taken many beatings in his short time on earth. He was already an old hand at withstanding pain. His skin had to be like leather. His mother's words shocked me.

"I'm bringin' tears to your eyes, boy, before this is over, if it takes all day." The fourth lick from the board hit Bull on his back and he fell to the floor. I jumped up to stop her.

"That's enough. Please stop." The next swing of the board hit Bull in the back of his head. He crawled across the office floor toward the far corner of the room as she moved with him still swinging. I was able to reach her before she could hit him the fifth time. I took the board away from her and my actions surprised and enraged her even more. She lost total control of herself as she pulled off one of her shoes and continued the beating with the new weapon. I took the shoe from her, trying to end the abuse I had become part of, but it continued to another level when she grabbed the American flag off the wall and began stabbing Bull with the pointed end of the pole. I had to physically pull her off the child and hold her against the wall.

The office staff alerted Mrs. McWilliams about the confrontation in my office. As usual, she came to assist me. She took Marcus into her office and out of harm's way. She calmed him and checked him for serious injuries. Ms. Haley sat down and I could see the rage had not left her. Her heavy breathing signaled her fatigue. She looked to be in another dimension. I was afraid of her. She could not seem to recover and return to the reality of my office. I told her I would have to report such abuse to the authorities. She looked at me as if I was the next one to take her abuse and in a slow and deliberate voice, complete with clenched teeth, the trade mark of the crazies, she made her thoughts clear to me.

"You want me to come here and make him be good in school, but you want to tie my hands when I do what has to be done." I was surprised at her ability to speak so clearly.

"Your methods are far too severe and you could really hurt him."

"Call who ever you want, just don't call me. If he needs a beatin' he's gettin' a beatin'. Don't you call me no more." She left my office and didn't take the boys with her. Ms. Haley didn't have to tell me not to call her. I already knew I would never call Bull's mother again. The HRS workers picked up Marcus the Bull and his brother Robert that afternoon. They were returned to their mother that same night.

On another occasion, I was talking to Bull's brother, Robert, in my office. Bull's teacher had seen a bad bruise on the child's arm and had reported it to Mrs. McWilliams. I wanted to talk to Robert first, to see if he knew anything about how his little brother got the big bruise. Robert told me he didn't think the bruise was from any beating Marcus had received at home lately. He thought it was from the two of them playing tackle football in the neighborhood. I was sure the two boys played rough and he was probably telling the truth about the origin of the bruise on Marcus' arm. I was about to tell Robert to go back to class, when he decided to share a story with me. It was obvious he was ready to talk and wanted me to know.

"Bull's last real bad beatin' was two weeks ago. I don't get bad beatin's no more, like I used to. Bull gets 'em now. He don't know when to be quiet. He always says somethin' back to Mama or Daddy and then he really gets it. I tell him to shut up, but he don't listen."

"So you know how to keep from getting in trouble at home? You need to keep trying to help Bull so he won't get those bad beatings."

"The last time he got it from Daddy, me and Mama listened at the bedroom, while he was getting' it. He was yellin' and Daddy was yellin' and hittin'. I was scared I would be next."

"What did your mother say when she heard Bull?"

"She just said, 'save me a piece of him'." I let Robert go back to class.

Granny Gown

Joining the teacher assistants for cafeteria duty during breakfast was not my favorite activity in the morning, but the children did seem to behave better with me down there. When you feed as many as five hundred students a free breakfast before school you welcome any and all adult supervision you can get. The line for breakfast reminded me of Disney World when I waited in line to see the Country Bear Jamboree. The morning breakfast line was about that long and it always amazed me. I was wiping off one of the cafeteria tables when Melissa, a fifth grade patrol, came running into the cafeteria. When I saw Melissa's facial expression I knew something was very wrong.

"Mr. Reynolds, come quick! There's a lady with red hair grabbing kids and pulling them into the bushes by the sidewalk. She pushed me down and made me eat a cigarette."

Now, not much surprised me anymore, but I didn't want that to be true. However, Melissa was our only gifted student in the school and I was sure something had really scared her. I hurried and followed her so she could show me what she was talking about. As we walked together, three other students approached us complaining about the red headed lady making them eat cigarettes. One boy still had tobacco on the side of his face as he told me what happened. I had no idea what I was getting ready to find and I didn't like the possibilities. We had only walked a block from the school when Melissa stopped and pointed to a single large bush next to the sidewalk in front of us.

"There she is, Mr. Reynolds. See her behind that bush?" Once again, I couldn't believe my eyes, but there she was, just like the students had said, squatting behind the bush. She had long red hair and looked to be in her thirties. She was barefoot and wearing a long flannel "granny" gown. I tried to shake the strange and unbelievable vision from my head, but it was real and guess who had to deal with it. Remember, I was the principal.

The sidewalk was littered with cigarette papers and tobacco. The woman saw me and moved closer to the bush as if to hide even more. We stared at each other. Now, I was not gifted like Melissa, but it didn't take me long to figure out there was something seriously wrong with the red headed woman squatting behind that bush. My heart raced, as usual, in anticipation of a bizarre confrontation. I asked Melissa to direct the other students away from the lady in the bush and I asked another one of the students to go to the school and ask Mrs. Gilmer to call the police.

The patrol car must have been in the area because it pulled up in record time. I pointed the woman out to the young officer and explained to him what I thought had been happening. Another patrol car pulled up and the two officers walked cautiously toward the bush. She didn't move as the two men approached her. It was as if she didn't think they could see her as long as she was hiding behind the bush. Both officers stepped behind the bush and each took her by an arm, picking her up off the ground. She didn't say or do anything. She just let them move her to the back seat of one of the patrol cars. I walked back to the school with the students who had gathered to watch the excitement.

Minutes later, the police car drove up to the front of the school. I met the officer and he questioned me about the incident. He said the lady had no identification and there was, no doubt, something wrong with her. I'm not sure how to tell the rest of this story, but things got absolutely crazy.

The redhead had some kind of body seizure. She began kicking the windows of the patrol car and beating her head against the protective screen. She stood up in the seat, pulled up her granny gown, exposing the fact she wore no underwear, pushed the front of her body against the window and urinated on the glass. The young police officer used his shoulder radio to call for assistance as the bizarre rage continued in the back seat of his patrol car.

Then she added insult to the insanity when she pulled her gown up again and pushed her buttocks against the same window and...well I won't say it, but it was an awful moment and scene. The police officer looked at me and for a moment there was a male bonding of amazement and disbelief. It was easy to see the young officer didn't know what to do. I was sure he was not getting into the car. It even got worse, if you can imagine, when she began to finger paint on the window. More police officers arrived and they were shocked at what they saw. The officers discussed their options, but none included getting into the car with the woman. They would wait for the rescue truck and the medical team.

I was called to the office as the rescue unit arrived. A student had fallen and injured his arm. I checked to see if it was broken. It was. The child's mother was called and I returned to the wild scene outside the school. Again, I was amazed.

The police car was empty, all the doors were open and the odor was nauseating. The redheaded woman lay tied down on a stretcher in the back of the rescue truck. What ever they had decided had done the trick. One of the officers got into the car; doors still wide open, and drove it onto a grassy area away from the school building. Our custodian hooked up a water hose and helped the officer wash the inside of the car the best they could. The police car remained on campus most of that day, but just before school was dismissed, a tow truck hauled it away.

Star and The Pirate

When I decided to take Joey home that day, it was to give us some relief and to try and meet his mother. Joey was a sun tanned little knot of a boy. Even his arms had a muscular dimension to them that was unusual for a child his age. He wasn't as handsome as Maurice, but he had a great look for a little boy. They had no phone and all of our attempts to contact her had failed. Joey was the worst of her three children, but Phillip and Charles also created their share of trouble in and out of the classroom. Joey was my main concern that day because of his profane and improper language and that he had thrown a book across the classroom. He usually arrived at school angry in the mornings and pretty much stayed that way all day. Fun and light moments were few and far between if you dealt with Joey. Joey's younger brother, Charles, was not in school that day. The older brother, Phillip, was in class. I had to ask Phillip for the proper directions to find where they lived. I knew Joey would never lead me to the correct address. When Phillip gave me the information I realized they lived only a few streets east of the school. I took Joey home.

The trailer was on a dirt lot. Joey's younger brother, Charles, was playing in the dirt near the steps and front door of the singlewide trailer. Charles stood up when we drove up in my Volkswagen. He jumped over a large pit bull, which was lying on the ground, and ran to the trailer door. The dog stood up, but it didn't bark. Even with no barking, I still wasn't too crazy about getting out of the car. I've already expressed my feelings about devil dogs. I was very cautious and watched the dog as Joey and I walked to the door. Little brother, Charles, was yelling and banging on the door.

"Mama! Mama! Mr. Reynolds's here with Joey." The door didn't open right away and Charles continued his frantic banging. After about a full minute of waiting and banging the door opened. I couldn't see anyone standing in the doorway. I moved closer, watching the dog as it watched me. I was already sorry I had taken Joey home and I really hated that dog. There was movement in the doorway. Someone was sitting in a wheelchair and was struggling to open the door. I wasn't sure if it was a man or a woman. The person was dressed in black, with high, black boots. The boots had chains wrapped around them and the individual had a black patch over the right eye. I thought perhaps I had missed the party. Each time I think I am at the point in my career where nothing can surprise me, something does. It was a scary human being and I was uneasy once again. It greeted me, I think.

"What do you want?" The voice was deep and raspy, but I still wasn't sure if I had encountered a woman or a man. The voice didn't make guessing any easier.

"I'm Mr. Reynolds, from the school. I have Joey with me and I need to talk to his mother."

"What's the little shit done now?" I was so sorry I was there.

"He won't cooperate with us at school at all and he causes major disturbances all over. I really need your help."

"You don't need my help. He ain't mine. If he was mine, you wouldn't be havin' all this trouble with him. I'll get his mother. Just wait here." It looked back toward the front room of the trailer and yelled: "Star, it's a man from the school with Joey." The wheelchair moved away from the door allowing Joey's mother, Star, to step up into the doorway.

"What's wrong now, Mr. Reynolds." Once again I couldn't believe my eyes. His mother was dressed in all black, like the pirate in the wheelchair, boots and all. She had long raven black hair and she was very pretty. In fact, she was beautiful by any standard. I tried not to stare at her or look shocked at her appearance, but I did.

"Are you Joey's mother?"

"Yes, I'm Star Harris. He's mine, I'm sometimes sad to say." I needed to get my mind on the duty at hand, but Star had my full attention. I fought my way back to the reality of the situation.

"Mrs. Harris, we cannot control Joey at school. We would like to test him and get to the bottom of the problem. We have a fine testing program that will give us information as to why he is having such difficulty. It is very hard to get in touch with you so this seemed like the best way to contact you." The pirate hollered from inside the trailer.

"He don't need no test. That's for crazy kids. He just needs his ass beat." The voice reminded me of the character, Swamp Witch Hattie, as it cracked in the distance. I assumed it was a woman's voice, but I still wasn't sure. I knew it was crazy no matter what it was. Star paid no attention to the statement and continued the conversation.

"Mr. Reynolds, I have serious problems with Joey, too. If these tests can help I'm willing to talk to you about them. If you would like to come in we can talk here now, or I'll meet you at school, if that would be better for you.

"I really need to get back to school." I was almost hypnotized by her calm and kind words, as well as her appearance. It didn't seem to fit. Like I said, it was crazy. She added more information.

"You need to know more about my boys, especially Joey. They have not had things very easy and I think you need to know more about them." The pirate joined in again.

"You don't need to tell him nothin'. Just tell him to send Joey home if he can't handle him. Ain't he 'sposed to take care of kids like Joey? What do we pay him for if he can't handle kids? Tell him to do his job at school and you'll do yours here." Again, Star didn't pay any attention to the noise behind her. I wanted to go into the trailer and slap what ever it was out of that wheelchair, but that was just an unprofessional fantasy.

"Mr. Reynolds, I'll meet you at school in fifteen minutes and we can talk without interruptions." I agreed and watched the dog as I left. I couldn't wait to talk to Star Harris. Fifteen minutes later she was sitting in my office.

She was dressed like the rock star, Stevie Nicks. I think it was a gothic style. She had even added a black-laced shawl to her attire. When she started talking it was true confession at its finest.

"Mr. Reynolds, all three of my boys have been sexually abused by adults. Joey was the most abused and he had some awful things happen to him. The man who abused him is in prison now for that abuse. He was my boyfriend at the time. Phillip and Charles were abused by a young man who lived next door to us in Georgia. He was our babysitter from time to time. They are not normal because of the abuse they have suffered." Then she went into her personal woe.

Her name was Linda Harris, but Star was her stage name when she danced. She was a topless dancer at the local tavern. All three of her boys had different fathers and none of the boys had ever seen their fathers. She was four months pregnant with Phillip when his father was stabbed and killed in a bar fight in Georgia. They were going to get married that same week, but it never happened. Joey's father was a construction worker she had danced for in the club one night. She took him home with her after she got off work and they spent the weekend together. He left early the next Monday morning for work and he asked her to bring him some lunch at noon. She said she really did like him and was excited about taking his lunch to him. When she arrived at the job site and asked for him, she was told he had been injured in a fall from a scaffold and had been taken to the hospital. When she entered the emergency room she was told he was dead. Nine months later Joey was born. She said she knew he would have been a good man to have a baby with. His name was Joe, but his child was called Joey.

"He looks a lot like his daddy. I didn't get to go to Joe's funeral 'cause they flew his body back to Texas where he was from." Even though I'm sure I had a dumbfounded look on my face, she continued. "Charles' father was a truck driver; eighteen wheeler. Big truck, big man. He was crazy about me and the two boys. He wasn't the best lookin' man I ever slept with, but he took good care of us. I didn't dance when I was with him. That's how I judge men. If they don't want me to keep dancin', then I know they are interested in me. If they still allow me to dance, then I know they are after one thing and I don't stay with them. I get what I can from them, just like they are doing to me. When I found out I was carryin' Charles, we married ourselves that night. That's all we needed. Two weeks later he fell asleep at the wheel of his truck and he was gone. About six months later Charles was born. Three boys, three dead daddies. That's crazy, ain't it?"

I didn't know what to say so I waited, hoping she would continue. "I think it all changed me and made me crazy too. I still dance, but no more men. Me and men are just too dangerous. Kelly's all I need now." I took for granted Kelly was the pirate in the wheelchair at the trailer. I didn't ask. I just listened. "I wanted you to know about my boys, so maybe you would understand a little more when you have trouble with them."

"I'll do my best to work with your boys." It wasn't much, but it was all I could say. My head was still spinning from her tale. I never saw Star again, but I did see Swamp Witch Hattie sign the boys out of school early one day. I watched her roll down the street with the boys walking along side of the wheelchair. We later had to make a report to the HRS because Joey had been beaten with a belt buckle and he came to school with cuts on his legs and shoulders. After the HRS made contact with Ms. Harris she and the boys moved back to Georgia. People with those types of behavior and such backgrounds always seem to stay on the run.

Intimidation

My second encounter with Sally's mother came to ruin another of my days. The devil was at hand. Sally came to school with an awful black eye that was swollen shut. It was as if the evil one wanted us to see the injured eye and offer a challenge to us. That's the way I looked at it, anyway.

Sally's teacher, Mrs. Keller, brought Sally to my office right away and we called the abuse registry again. Sally would not talk to us at all; she only stared straight ahead with her one good, adult looking eye. She looked pitiful and the eye looked painful and serious. Ms. Mc Williams checked Sally for other marks or injuries, but she only had a few small bruises on her legs. Children often have such bruises on their legs from everyday play.

Our emergency call to the abuse registry brought the HRS worker out to the school in about two hours. It was a different person than the time before. I explained my concerns again. Sally was still not talking, so the HRS representative left Sally with us and made a visit to the devil woman. She was gone about fifteen minutes. Not a good sign for Sally or us.

Mrs. Dalton told the HRS worker that Sally would not talk because the child was scared of the principal at school and Sally's eye was hurt when a top bunk bed support fell on her while she and her brother were jumping on the bed. Mrs. Dalton promised to take Sally to the doctor and have her eye examined. Sally was allowed to go home that day. I wasn't pleased with the HRS visit, but once again I could do nothing. I was ready to end the day and go home, but no such luck. Remember, I was the principal.

"Hey, you cocksucker, I got somethin' for ya." My heart went wild when I heard that devil's voice and looked up from my desk to see the evil Mrs. Dalton. I just knew she had a gun and was going to shoot me. I stood up quickly. She remained at the doorway of my office. "You're gonna learn to mind your own business and leave us alone. Your first lesson will be today. It usually don't take more than one lesson." I wanted to run. But I didn't think my legs would move. She added to my fears.

"I want you to meet my friend, Charlie. He's gonna break both your legs." At that frightening statement, a huge monster of a man stepped into the doorway, or should I say, became the doorway. Mrs. Dalton moved into the office so I could get the full view of the monster. He actually filled the doorway. He looked like a refrigerator with a head. It was an incredible sight for a school principal to deal with. Once again, I couldn't remember taking a class that prepared me for what I was facing at that moment. I was alone with no one to call the police for me. Everyone had gone home and the custodians were in another part of the building. I honestly thought I was going to die at the hands of the devil woman and her monster. She commanded her mutant companion.

"Bust him up, Charlie!" For some reason, with me standing, Charlie hesitated a second after her command. Perhaps it took that long for her words to register in his little prehistoric pea brain. When he hesitated I saw my possible salvation. There was a baseball bat leaning against the wall next to my desk. I had taken it from a student a few days before. We didn't allow wooden bats at school. Someone always gets hurt in elementary school if there's a wooden bat around. I was glad to see the bat at that particular time. I heard that Clint Eastwood movie music I had come to know so well and I picked up the wooden bat. I was inspired as I stepped from behind my desk and became the aggressor, holding the bat up high in the direction of Mrs. Dalton, who was the closest one to me. I will never forget what I said. To this day I can't believe it.

"Charlie, if you take one step, I will hit her in the head with this bat." I shocked myself with that statement. It was easy to see my two visitors couldn't believe it either, but Charlie must have taken me at my word because he didn't move. Mrs. Dalton moved away from me into the corner of the room, but I moved with her ready to swing the wood.

"Charlie, you have ten seconds to leave or I'll start swinging this thing." I was again amazed when Charlie started to back out of the doorway. The devil woman was mad.

"You chickenshit!" I was sure she was talking to Charlie. "He ain't gonna hit nobody. He's the damn principal. He can't hit nobody." I didn't know what to do next. I heard the front door close, so I hoped Charlie, like Elvis, had left the building. I continued holding the bat in the attack position over Mrs. Dalton. I wanted to hit her so bad. It would have ended a great deal of future suffering for many, but that was just an unrealistic thought on my part during a weak moment. Her defiance, as the bat threatened her, gave proof of her insanity.

"You hit me and I'll have your job. You're in big trouble for even tryin' to hit me. You must be crazy." I had no words for the mentally disturbed woman. I don't remember my thoughts at all. I just wanted it all to be over.

She moved past me toward the door. I could see a moment of fear in her eyes and I liked her being afraid. I wanted her to feel it. She left and I locked the main building. I watched her get into a truck with Charlie and I could hear her yelling at him as they drove away, but I couldn't hear what she was saying. I called security and told them about the scary incident and that I was going home. I would write the report in the morning.

A few days after the bat incident and my introduction to Charlie, I was preparing to visit the cafeteria, when our school clerk, Mrs. Highsmith, came to my office door.

"Mr. Reynolds, you have a parent here who would like to see you." Now, at that particular time in my educational career, those were not pleasant words for me. Such words created that unnerving, irregular heart beat in my chest. I took a deep breath and forced myself not to judge all parents because of a few bad apples. I needed to remember that an elementary school should be a fun place to be. I tried not to be on guard, but I couldn't help it. A small man, probably in his fifties, walked into my office. He looked like an American Indian. He had dyed jet-black hair with a long ponytail hanging down his back. For some reason I noticed his hands. They were covered with dirt and grease exactly like Mrs. Dalton's hands had been. I didn't like the feeling I was having at all. I stood up and I knew I wouldn't shake his hand. He made me nervous and I had become very tired of being on guard all the time. I proceeded, like the public servant I was supposed to be.

"Good morning sir, I'm Bill Reynolds, how may I help you this morning?" No problem with the handshake. He didn't offer. The Indian did offer me the information I did not need to know.

"I'm Sally's father and we need to talk." I liked my situation less and less, but I didn't want him to see my discomfort. I was getting very good at not showing my fear.

"Please sit down, sir." He seemed calm and I waited for him to begin.

"I want to end all the problems we're havin' here at school. I hope we can get this stuff worked out. It's getting' out of hand, don't ya think?" He seemed reasonable, but I had been wrong before. I'm sure paranoia comes in part from experiences.

"Mr. Dalton, Sally is being hurt at home and your wife even brought a man here to hurt me."

"If I thought my wife was hurtin' Sally I'd throw her out, myself. I love Sally and ain't lettin' nothin' happenin' to her. She's a happy child. I'm sorry my wife's been actin' so stupid. She always carries things too far. She won't bother you again, I promise." I recognized an empty promise when I heard one, as he added more.

"If you think Sally is being hurt, you call me and let me know. I've been drivin' a school bus for years and I don't want no child to be hurt, any child.

Mr. Dalton also told me that during the day, between his bus runs, he worked at a car repair garage near the school and he gave me the telephone number at the shop so I could reach him if I needed to talk to him. It was very difficult to trust anyone who was married to the devil woman.

I had seen Ms. Green a number of times before in the mornings around the school, but I had not met her. I knew Mrs. McWilliams was working with her two boys, Hoss and Jamie, trying to control their continual misbehavior at school. Most of the school's contact with her had been through Mrs. McWilliams. When Ms. Green said she wanted to see me, I thought it was about her boys.

"Good morning, Ms. Green, is there something I can help you with?"

"No, Mr. Reynolds, but I think you should know what happened last night." She could see I was listening as she continued. "I was invited to a party last night at the Dalton's house." My heart quivered and I felt my blood flow change directions at the mention of the troll. "There was about ten people there. All had children in your school. The reason for the get together was to talk about you. Mrs. Dalton wants us all to get all our friends to write letters complaining about you. She told us she knows about your past as a devil worshiper. She told us they found children dead on the playground of the other schools you have worked in. I don't believe none of what she said and I just thought you should know how crazy that woman really is. She's always been crazy, but a lot of people around here listen to her because they're scared of her and her husband. He might be the crazier of the two. Some folks think she can work Voo Doo or Black Magic. She's always talkin' about puttin' spells on people. I think she says all that stuff to keep people scared of her. She really likes to scare people. She's a mean one, but I don't believe in none of that foolishness." My head started spinning again and the day had just begun. I needed to thank her for the strange and disturbing information.

"I really do appreciate you telling me this. Mrs. Dalton told me she would get me fired. I guess this is the beginning of her effort to do so."

"Well, just you be careful. That's one crazy family."

She left me to think about the new information, but I didn't know what to do about it. I let it go for the moment and took on the regular school business. That afternoon, it all surfaced once again when a reporter from a local television station called me and asked if he could come to the school and take pictures of the human bones we had found on the playground. Were people crazy, or what?

The Babysitter

During the days that followed my meeting with Ms. Green, a number of other parents told me tales that Mrs. Dalton was spreading about me in the community. I informed   school board security about the problem I was having and I wanted the information recorded. With the media calling me, it was easy to surmise the rumors were getting out of hand and becoming a serious problem for me. I hoped the reasonable parents would realize how crazy Mrs. Dalton actually was and the stories about me were coming from her evil imagination and her desire for vengeance.   I didn't like the situation and it did bother me.

I began to notice that during the week, a white Volkswagen was picking up Sally after school each day. She had usually walked home. The driver was a young man in his early twenties. I planned to call Sally into my office the next morning, but I didn't have to, Mrs. McWilliams brought her to me.

Sally's teacher, Ms. Keller, wanted us to see a cut behind Sally's ear. When I saw the cut I knew it should have had stitches. I got mad, but puzzled that Mrs. Dalton would send Sally to school with such a horrible injury. I knew the woman was crazy, but it was still hard to understand. Was it another challenge and show of contempt at Sally's expense? I was hoping that wasn't the case. I detested that vile excuse for a mother bad enough.

"Sally, has your mother seen this cut?" She shook her head, no. "How did it happen?" She looked down and remained silent. I recognized her silent treatment from before. I had to press her that time and it was still no use.

"Sally, we can't help you if you don't talk to us. You don't have to be hurt like this all the time." She didn't look up.

"Mama didn't do it. Jimmy did it." I couldn't believe she said that.

"Who's Jimmy?"

"He baby sits me." She still didn't lift her head.

"Is he the one picking you up in the little punch-bug?" She smiled when I said "punch-bug", but still kept her head down.

"Yes, sir."

"Sally, what happened?" I was pleased as she started to talk. Her head was still down, but she was talking. "We were play wrestlin'. We always play wrestlin'. Jimmy held me up in the air by my feet. He was swingin' me back and forth, ringing me like a bell. He did it for a long time and it scared me 'cause I couldn't breathe. When I screamed he dropped me on the coffee table in the living room. I hit my head. It was my fault for being such a baby and screamin'." That was the most I had ever heard Sally talk. I was actually very sad with regard to the nature and subject matter of our first real conversation. Sally needed help and I knew she was counting on me. Her adult looking eyes said that to me loud and clear. I couldn't believe she kept talking.

"It was bleedin' bad and I was cryin'. There was drips on the floor, but Jimmy cleaned them up before Mama got home."

"Did you tell your mother?"

"No sir. When I stopped cryin' he gave me a pill, so I would feel better. I went to sleep. I think he told Mama when she got home."

"What did your mother say to you this morning?"

"Nothin', she was sleepin' too hard. I got dressed and came to school. I didn't want to miss breakfast. I didn't eat last night."

Mrs. McWilliams called Mrs. Dalton and told her about Sally's story and injury. She requested that Sally be taken to the doctor. Only minutes after Mrs. McWilliams had made the phone call the white Volkswagen pulled up to the front of the school. Mrs. Dalton had sent Jimmy, the babysitter from hell, to get Sally. I couldn't believe it. I was sick to my stomach. Even after Mrs. McWilliams had told the mother what Sally had said, she still didn't care. I called Mrs. Dalton to express my concern and reluctance to allow Sally to leave with the young man, but she insisted and once again let me know it was none of my business. She said it was an accident and that was the end of it. We reported the incident to the HRS again. Sally missed three days of school.

The Golden Crucifix Knife

The very next day I was called to the fourth grade wing of the school because we had another intruder. When I entered the area, I saw a thinly built and frail looking woman standing outside one of the classrooms. Her skin was snow white and she had dark circles under her eyes. Her emaciated face had high cheekbones and her eyes were sunk back in the head. She had long gray hair and was wearing a black, sheer ankle length dress. She was reaching to open one of the classroom doors. I had to get her attention.

"Excuse me. May I help you?" I was shocked when she turned around. She honestly looked like a real witch. She even had a wart on her nose. She really scared me and I'm sure my obvious fear was easy for her to detect. My fright increased when I saw the large, Bowie long bladed hunting knife that she held in her hand. The witch had a wild look on her face and I became afraid for all of us. The knife looked as if it were solid gold. Although she was not holding it in a threatening manner, the fact she held it in her hand was enough to scare me. I wanted to draw her attention away from the classroom.

"I'm sorry ma'am, but we don't allow visitors to walk around the school without a pass from the office. Please come with me and we can get you a visitor's pass." The witch stood there and stared at me with crazy eyes as if I was the crazy one there on the sidewalk. She did have a point, though, after my "you need a visitor's pass" statement. But at least she didn't enter the classroom and her advance down the sidewalk had been interrupted for the moment. I needed to continue to talk to her.

"Is there something I can help you with? Are you O.K.?" She whispered in a calm and strange voice. The evil ones always seem to have strange and dramatic voices.

"I was told I could find the devil here."

I felt the blood flowing in my veins change directions again. It was becoming a common occurrence and sensation for me. It was true, what was said about being afraid and one's blood running cold. For some reason in my cold state I found words coming out of my icy lips.

"I don't think what you have heard is true. There is no devil here." Now, was that stupid or what? I couldn't believe I said, "There is no devil here". I think I used my best evil voice, too. I was caught up in the drama. She had more to say.

"I came here to introduce the devil to Jesus. The devil, who hurts children." I knew at that moment, Mrs. Dalton's tales of my association with the devil had hit a serious nerve with the strange individual I was facing at the moment. She continued. "I have this to show the devil." She lifted the knife up over her head, holding the blade in her hand, exposing the handle. I stepped back just in case she thought she had seen the devil and that I was the object of her position of attack. Ironically, the handle of the knife she held was a beautiful golden crucifix. I had never seen such a knife. The woman held it up reverently with both of her hands.

"Jesus wants us to protect the children." She lowered the knife. Then, to my amazement, she turned away from me and ran across the schoolyard and out to the public playground area next to the back fence of the school. A number of teachers joined me as I watched her running. The police had been called. They supposedly were on the way. Then, I was shocked once more when one of our fourth grade boys walked up to me. I was still thinking of how to protect the children. I snapped at the young boy.

"Don't come out here! Go back to your classroom and tell your teacher no one is to leave the room. Tell her to lock the door." The child looked up at me.

"Mr. Reynolds, that's my mom out there. She's been real bad sick and she don't live with us no more. She ain't 'spose to be around here."

The police arrived, approached the lady on the playground and took her away. I was sure she had hunted the devil before. I wondered why she hadn't found Mrs. Dalton. That night someone found the dead body of a newborn baby in the dumpster at the apartment complex near the school. It was the topic of conversation the next morning.

Boy Scout Leader from Hell

I first saw Alvin Lester, as he sat on a little BMX racing bicycle blocking one of the school buses from exiting from the bus-loading zone. He was thin, but a muscular young man. His arms looked like tight cables. He had uncombed straw colored hair that touched his shoulders and fell across his eyes. It was easy to see the young man didn't smile very much. When I asked him to move he stared at me for a second or so and then he reluctantly moved and demonstrated his defiance by racing down the school sidewalk. He was making other students move out of his path as they were walking to the bus loading area. I didn't understand and I didn't like his behavior. He looked to be in his late teens, but his actions didn't seem to fit his age and size. He had ridden out of my sight and I thought he had left the school grounds. I concentrated on the bus riders and dismissing the other students.

As the last bus pulled away, I saw him again. He was still sitting on his bicycle, but now he was on the outside of the school fence. I watched him as he watched me. He took his disrespect and defiance to a higher level when he got off the bike and began to throw rocks over the fence into the school parking lot. He was talking as he threw the rocks, but I couldn't understand what he was saying. After a few moments of the bombing, I removed his target when I walked back into the building. He was gone when I went out to my car to go home. I was glad he didn't see me get into my car and I hated the fact that he would probably find out later that it was mine.

I returned to school that same night for our Boy Scout roundup. It was an annual event in the county schools that helped the scouting organizations recruit new members and give information to the children and their parents about the upcoming scouting activities. I had only spoken to our school scoutmaster on the telephone. I had not met him yet. He was going to be at the roundup with his troop in full dress. His name was Mr. Dudley.

Mr. Dudley arrived early to meet me and to set up registration tables for anyone interested in joining the scouts. As soon as I shook his hand and smelled his breath I knew Mr. Dudley had been drinking. A small number of parents attended, but I knew even a small group would be able to see his condition. I recognized some of our students when the scouts began coming into the cafeteria. I was especially pleased to see Tommy Lude dressed in his scout uniform. Mrs. McWilliams had been working with Tommy because of his poor self-concept and it was nice to see him active in something positive. I would have never guessed Tommy was a Boy Scout.

Tommy's mother had shaved his head because of his head lice. Shaving the head seemed to be the cure of choice for the infected families in the neighborhood. Just shave the head and then it's easy to see those little rascals. Because of the curvature of his spine, Tommy wore a metal back brace that also supported his neck. His clothes never fit him and they were always dirty and stained. Tommy was in the third grade, but he was supposed to be in the fifth. He was much too big to be with third graders and was often the butt of jokes and teasing.

Tommy had every reason to be withdrawn, so Mrs. McWilliams was trying to create a more positive atmosphere for him at school. It was obvious he didn't have the best home life. At least we could try to help Tommy when he was at school with us. Even though his uniform didn't fit, it was still nice to see Tommy standing there with the other scouts.

I spent the early part of the meeting introducing myself to the parents and telling Tommy how proud I was of him. It was time for the pledge to the flag and the official start of the evening activities. Troop leader Dudley marched his scouts onto the stage and they stood at attention when they stopped. They were not the most polished group of scouts I had seen, but they were very serious about their moment on the stage. The room was silent as Mr. Dudley motioned to one of the older scouts. The young man stepped forward and began the pledge to the flag. All in the cafeteria followed his lead.

"I pledge allegiance, to the flag….."

As the voices came together with the words of the pledge, I couldn't believe my eyes. The young man leading the pledge was the same defiant youngster who sat on his BMX bicycle and threw rocks at me that same afternoon. Not only was he a scout in our school troop, he was a troop leader and Mr. Dudley's assistant.

The thought of Mr. Dudley and that awful young man teaching our students how to be good citizens made me sick. It could not continue. I asked Mr. Dudley to meet with me in the morning. He said he would call me. The round up ended and I went home.

It was so difficult not to take my work home with me. For my sanity, I had always tried to leave emotions and circumstance at the job site. I tried not to think about Mr. Dudley and his scouts, but I was upset and the thoughts stayed with me. I wanted no part of having him at my school. I couldn't wait for the next morning and my meeting with Mr. Dudley. Again, I was wishing my time away. Why did I do that?"

The next day I decided to find out more about our scouts before I talked to Mr. Dudley. I called Tommy Lude and some of the other scouts I had seen at the round up to my office. I was curious about the activities of the scouts under Dudley's care. Once the boys started talking, they gave me more information than I expected. I was overwhelmed with the statements they made to me. They told me more than I actually wanted to hear. Tommy was the most vocal. He knew I would listen. Whatever Mrs. McWilliams was doing to help Tommy, it was working. He just needed to know someone was on his side.

The name of the young man leading the pledge was Alvin Lester. He was seventeen years old and had dropped out of school. Alvin stayed with Mr. Dudley sometimes. Bobby told me that during two camping trips, Mr. Dudley instructed Alvin to give each boy a small sip of Jack Daniels whiskey. Mr. Dudley had said it would help the boys to fall asleep and to keep the mosquitoes away. Were people crazy, or what?

I was also told that if any of the scouts misbehaved or could not tie the knot of the week, they would be forced to run through a belt gauntlet made up of the members of the troop, including Mr. Dudley. Mr. Dudley also had a rule that the boys would settle all disputes and arguments by putting on old boxing gloves and fighting it out. The boys hadn't talked very long, but I had heard enough. I sent them back to class. While I was learning about the scouts, Mr. Dudley called and left me a message that he would see me after school. I couldn't wait to see the Scout Master from hell.

Even though I was preparing myself for the meeting with Mr. Dudley I still had to take care of the school business at hand. One of my problems that day was to deal with a mistake I had made weeks before. Our fund raising attempts were disastrous in a school where the majority of the student body consisted of students from households supported by the welfare system. It was difficult to sell anything to parents. They just didn't have the money for extras. We had made an attempt at selling candy bars. How I let that salesman talk me into that, I'll never know. Sometimes those salesmen catch you at a weak moment and they can talk you into anything. Maybe we just needed to try one more time. Let's add another huge mistake to my sizable collection of poor judgments.

I allowed the students and parents to take the candy home to sell it. Unfortunately, however, if they sold it at all, they ended up keeping the money rather than turning it in to the school. We lost about a thousands dollars on the "fundraiser" that we had to pay back to the candy salesman.

We were also missing some of the money a few of our students had collected and actually turned in. I had to meet with a parent who was the P.T.A. treasurer to discuss the foiled candy sale and the missing money. During our meeting, to add to the sadness of the candy sale, the treasurer told me she had taken ninety dollars of the candy money and bought crack cocaine. She was sorry and ashamed, but she said she couldn't help it. That same day, Mrs. McWilliams assisted her in admitting herself into a drug rehab program in the area.

The other events of that day are not as strong in my mind as the problems with the candy sale and the true confession of the P.T.A. treasurer, but I do remember that afternoon when Mr. Dudley walked into my office as the last bus left the school.

Mr. Dudley wore a dirty t-shirt that looked three sizes too small, exposing his hairy watermelon belly. He smelled worse than he did at the scout round up and it was obvious he had been drinking again. He sat down and I immediately brought up the problems I was having with his being scoutmaster.

"Mr. Dudley, you can no longer be the scoutmaster at this school." He did not react to my words at all, so I continued. "You give the boys alcohol to drink, you have them beaten if they make mistakes, and you encourage them to settle problems by fighting. These actions are against everything scouting stands for." He still had no reaction as I went on. "You have been drinking with the students under your supervision. Both times I have seen you, you have also been drinking, including now. I have to protect these children. It's my job." He decided to join the one sided conversation.

"I've been doing this for eight years and you don't say who leads the scouts. We only use the school for our meetings."

"You will not be allowed to use this building anymore and I am going to contact the parents and inform them of your tactics." He didn't care at all.

"You can contact anybody you want. The mamas and daddies love me. They know I'll make men out of their little whimps."

"Good Bye, Mr. Dudley." He stood up and smiled at me as he walked toward the door.

"Are you a fag or somethin'?" I didn't respond so he figured he could continue his attempt at intimidation. "Didn't nobody ever tell you that real men settle differences eye-to-eye? A little Jack Daniels never hurt nobody. Maybe if you ran through a belt line when you was a boy you wouldn't be such a queen now."

Even though I knew better and I was supposed to be above such things, I found myself wanting to step outside with Mr. Dudley. I heard that Clint Eastwood music playing in my head again, but it faded as Mr. Dudley left my office.

After reporting Dudley to the Scouting Association I was very disappointed and surprised when he was allowed to remain the troop leader. He moved the boys to another location for their meetings. I was also disappointed when only two of the boys were taken out of the troop by their parents. Perhaps, we can't save them all. It becomes so difficult to keep trying. Were people crazy or what?

Penmanship

One day I was walking down the sidewalk by the first grade wing and I saw one of our students, Dennis, standing on the sidewalk with his back to me. Dennis had been giving us a few problems about coming to school. He was having difficulty academically and he had left school a number of times during the day. I knew Dennis was supposed to be in his class. As I came closer to him I realized he was urinating on the sidewalk. Thinking back, I wish I had remained silent until he finished his business.

"Dennis! What are you doing?" I don't know why I asked such a stupid question when I already knew what he was doing. He turned back to me and spread the last of it to his left and ran away from me down the sidewalk, zipping his pants as he ran. I had no desire to chase a first grader who ran as fast as Dennis. It was obvious that Dennis knew how to run. Dennis' teacher, Ms. Wills, stepped out of her classroom.

"Mr. Reynolds, was that Dennis?"

"Yes it was."

"He didn't come to class. I thought he was absent today."

"Well, that was him." I shook my head. "Actually, he left us a present." She looked puzzled at my remark as I walked to the wet area

of the sidewalk. I looked down and could not believe my eyes. Dennis
had written his first name on the sidewalk with his own urine. Each
letter was printed neatly except for the "s". I'm sure that happened
when I interrupted his liquid penmanship lesson. Ms. Wills stepped
close to me to see what I was looking at. It took her a second or so to
realize what he had done. I asked Ms. Wills to consider giving him a
grade for his effort. It was the first penmanship exercise he had
completed the entire week.

When Ms. Carter walked into my office I was not prepared for the
information she gave me. "My daughter, Ellie, has been sexually
molested at this school." My heart jumped and like I said, I was not
prepared at all for her disturbing news.

"By an adult or another student?" I didn't know what a proper
response was so that would have to do for the moment.

"It was a student in her class."

"What class is she in?"

"Ms. Ford's class."

Now, at that point I realized we were talking about a child in our
four-year-old Pre-Kindergarten class.

"Your daughter is in Pre-K?"

"Yes, she was violated on the building block table and the teacher
saw it all. She must be a pervert. She just watched."

"Ms. Carter, I want to find out what has happened, but we are not
talking about seniors in high school. We are talking about four year old
babies."

"Well, he made her have sex on that table and I'm calling the police.
All I want from you is his mother's phone number so I can call her and
tell her she will be hearing from my lawyer and this school will too."

"Ms. Carter, I also find it hard to believe Ms. La Forty watched this
take place without stopping it. Don't you?" She didn't like what I was
saying.

"My husband, well he ain't my husband, but we been together long
enough, said you wouldn't believe it. You would try to cover it up.

So, just give me the phone number and I won't bother you again. We'll take care of it ourselves without you."

"Ms. Carter, I have to look into this first. And I can't give you another parent's phone number. I wouldn't give your number to a stranger. I'm sure you must understand that. If you tell me what happened, I will talk to Ms. Ford and the other parent. You have to allow me the time to investigate this situation, but I cannot give you the phone number." She was disgusted with me.

"He was right again. He said you wouldn't help us. He's a smart man."

I knew I was talking to another crazy one, but I tried to stay as professional as she would allow. This was a professionalism I would soon drift away from.

"Mr. Reynolds, I'm takin' Ellie to the doctor and if there has been any penetration this school is in serious trouble and so are you."

"Ms. Carter, even if something did happen in the class, I'm sure a complete sex act did not occur. The examination she will receive may be more traumatic than the actual incident in the classroom. Please let me look into this before you do anything else. Do you think perhaps the boy touched her or said something to her?"

"You don't believe it happened. Just give me the number."

"No, I won't do that." Her disgust was growing.

"Well, I was afraid of this. Now, you need to know about my husband. I thought I could keep him from coming here. If I don't go home with that number, he will come up to this school and do his own number on your ass. I'm supposed to tell you that." I didn't know what to say, so she took the moment to intimidate me some more.

"You've never met my husband. He will come up here and it won't be to talk or shake hands." She was really excited when she talked about her man. I figured our meeting was over.

"Good day, Ms. Carter."

After Ms. Carter left my office I talked to Ms. Ford and she had no idea what the woman was talking about. She knew of no problem at all. It wasn't long after I talked to Ms. Ford that I received a phone call.

"This is Bill Reynolds." The voice on the other end of the line was deep, slow and deliberate and with a low mean tone. I visualized the person talking with clenched teeth, the trademark of the intimidators and the bullies of the world.

"Bill, you...gonna...give...me...the...number?" I couldn't help it. I lowered my voice to match his.

"No." I was hoping the voice wouldn't sound so mean the next time I heard it, but I was wrong.

"If...I...come...up...there, you gonna be there?" It was an interesting question.

"Well, actually sir, I'd like to leave and not be here when you come, but I'll be here. I'm the principal. I have to be here." The intimidation continued.

"For your sake I hope you change your mind about that phone number before I get there." I was so sick of the fools I faced on a daily basis.

"I won't change my mind, sir." For some reason I wanted to see how stupid he would be. As the children say, "I started messin' with him."

"Sir, are you actually going to come here and beat me up if I don't give you the phone number?" I couldn't believe he answered me.

"If I have to, but I think you'll have a change of heart before I get there." I just couldn't let it end. At least if we were talking on the phone he wasn't beating me up.

"Would you do me a favor, sir?" He really was an idiot.

"What?"

"Could you beat me up outside so I'm not embarrassed in front of the ladies in the office? Could you at least do that?"

"Man, I don't care where you get your ass beat, but you're really startin' to piss me off big time."

"Okay then, I'll meet you at our bicycle rack out in front of the school. I'll be wearing a pink shirt." I'm not sure why I gave him my color of the day.

"Pink huh? My wife said you was a fag?" I needed to change something. They always call me a fag. He added to his insults. "I ain't rolled a queer in years." Not only was he going to beat me up, but he was going to take my money, too. He hung up. I had run out of talk and time.

I asked Mrs. Highsmith to call security and tell them a parent had threatened me and I thought he was coming to the school to hurt me. I don't know why, but I wanted to see how I would react to the confrontation. I took off my coat, so the pink shirt would be my calling card. Perhaps I was being brave because I knew security was on the way. I even took off my tie. For some reason, it seemed like the thing to do. My heart raced as usual, but it was more of an adrenalin rush. I think I was just tired of being the recipient of all the intimidation.

As a public servant and as the principal I had taken my share of abuse, but I wasn't going to that day. I lost what little professionalism I had for the moment. I picked up the baseball bat once again. The same bat that had protected me before was now a part of my office décor. I walked out into the main office. Mrs. Williams and Mrs. Highsmith gave me their usual concerned look. I nodded to them.

"I'm not sure what I'm doing. Be sure security is on the way just in case this man comes up here and shoots me." I walked outside to the bicycle rack where I was going to make my stand. I don't know why I was standing there. I was just so tired of the intimidation. I only stood there for a minute or so before a black Plymouth 'Cuda, with the front jacked up high, came rolling down the street. It was easy to see the driver of the car was still living in the early 70's, if you know what I mean.

The car pulled into the front circle driveway and stopped about thirty yards away from where I stood near the rack. He looked at me, but never turned off the car's engine. I held the baseball bat down next to my leg. I didn't lift it for him to see. As we looked at each other, I heard the music again. It kept me from running once more. It seemed to be a long stare down, but it was probably a short amount of time. Time moves slowly when fear and stress are involved. I couldn't believe my eyes when the 'Cuda began to move away slowly. He drove around the circle and left.

I just knew he had seen the bat and was going home to get his gun. I went back into the school to make sure someone from security was coming to assist me. Mr. Adam, a county detective, was near the school and would arrive within minutes. I cancelled the call to the police. Mr. Adam stayed with me the rest of the day, but the 'Cuda did not return.

The next morning I was on sidewalk duty. Principals at elementary schools have sidewalk duty, too. I saw Ms. Carter and her four-year-old daughter, Ellie, walking toward me. There was no doubt in my mind that she was looking for me. She walked up to me and stood there in her usual aggressive posture. I knew she was going to say something, so I waited for her.

"Well, you sure spit that phone number out when my husband jerked your butt over that desk of yours and slapped the shit out of you, didn't ya?" I couldn't believe my ears. I think I went into some kind of mild shock. I had to respond to her ridiculous statement.

"You mean, your husband told you he pulled me over my desk and slapped me?" She gave me a smile.

"Everybody in the neighborhood knows it. He's the talk of town." I know, as the principal I'm supposed to be above such things, but I just couldn't stand it.

"Ms. Carter, your husband never slapped me. In fact, he never even got out of his car. He's not the talk of the town. He's the liar of the town. He lied to you and everyone else." Her eyes lit up.

"I'm gonna tell him what you said. You just don't know when to quit, do ya? No matter what you say now, I have the phone number you gave him. That's all I wanted in the first place, but you had to do it the hard way." I still couldn't believe what I was hearing.

"Ms. Carter, did you call the number he gave you?"

"Yeah, but nobody's been home."

"Ms. Carter, nobody's ever going to be home at that number." Were people crazy, or what?

More Dirty Fingernails

When Sally Dalton returned to school the cut behind her ear was healing, but it was obvious the gash had never been stitched. That day I had a strange visitor. I knew the lady. She had been a school bus driver at another school where I worked before becoming the principal in Sin City. I would have an unbelievable headache before our wild conversation ended. I had been very fortunate during my life and had not been troubled with headaches like many other people I knew, but that day would be different. After a brief, "remember me?" introduction, she became very serious and poured her story on me.

She was Sally Dalton's half-sister, Betty. They had the same father. I had already met him. He was the greasy fingernails, American Indian school bus driver. Betty had been trying to get custody of Sally away from her father and her stepmother. The HRS had already taken one child away from them, because he had been locked in a closet and starved. There was also another child who was crippled and in a wheelchair because they failed to give him needed medication three years ago when he had some type of fever. The illness had caused brain damage. The child had been normal before the illness.

Betty said she had made complaints constantly to the HRS, but she was very disappointed at the lack of action by the protective

organization. She feared for Sally's safety. When she heard about the
problems we were having and the effort the school was making, she
thought we could help her get Sally away from her awful family and
the abuse.

I had never been very pleased with the support or action taken by
the HRS, but I was leery of her story about the other children. I would
take her words with caution, but I did want to hear more.

"They have done awful things to Sally, but their lies always seem to
keep them from getting in any trouble over what they do. Everybody's
scared of her and my father. They have hired real gangsters to hurt
people before. They have hired someone to break your legs as a
warning." I thought about the day Charlie stood at my office door. He
looked capable of breaking my legs. She had more "good" news. "My
father brags about being able to rig a car pipe bomb and he acts like he
has done it before." I was sick to my stomach and she still had more to
say. "You know she has a daycare business in their home?"
I couldn't believe my ears.

"You can't be serious." She was.

Betty told me she was surprised the HRS had given her stepmother
the license for a daycare in the home. At least six children, other than
Sally and her brother, stayed at the house each day. All the children
were handicapped in some way and had to wear braces or use
wheelchairs. They were all students who rode Mr. Dalton's school bus.
Instead of the children going home, they would stay at the Dalton's
house until their parents picked them up later in the day. One young
man in a wheelchair was sixteen years old. Sally was responsible for
feeding him and keeping him clean. She even gave him complete baths
when he soiled himself. This was a duty Betty felt was abusive for a
girl Sally's age. I agreed. Betty referred to her little half sister as a
child slave. The only life Sally had was at school and she wouldn't be
at school if it weren't for the law.

Betty told me that one night Sally knocked a pack of her mother's
cigarettes into a kitchen sink full of water while the child was washing

the dishes. The cigarettes got wet and ruined. Sally was forced to eat the wet cigarettes as her punishment for being so careless. When Betty confronted her stepmother about the punishment, Mrs. Dalton said she had caught Sally smoking and made her eat a cigarette so she wouldn't smoke again.

As another punishment, Sally had to sleep outside under the front porch during one of the coldest nights of the year wearing only her nightgown. Her toes cracked from the cold and bled during the night. Mrs. Dalton said Sally ran away and hid under the house and they didn't find her until morning. Sally told Betty the dog helped her stay warm.

Sally had to go to bed every night at seven o'clock. She was not allowed to leave her bedroom after that time. On one occasion, Sally told Betty she had tried very hard to stay in her room, but she had to go to the bathroom during the night. Sally had spent the day with an upset stomach and she couldn't control it. She had already soiled her panties so she took a chance, left her room and tried to make it to the toilet. The child relieved herself and began to wash her panties in the sink. Her mother caught her in the dark and made her eat what was left in the panties. Mrs. Dalton told Betty she didn't make Sally eat anything. She just rubbed the child's nose in the soiled panties like you would do a dog that made a mess on the floor. I couldn't listen to anymore of Betty's horror stories about the abuse Sally was suffering. True or not, I was finished for the day and I had another one of those unusual, but painful headaches.

When I arrived at school early the next morning, I stepped out the back door of the office to say good morning to our day custodian, Mr. Owens. He was a powerfully built young man and a good worker. I liked having him around. I was surprised when I learned he was a local ping-pong champion. I hadn't expected that. When I said, "good morning," he didn't respond to me and that was unusual. I could tell he was preoccupied with something, but I could not see what had his attention. He was looking down the sidewalk. I stepped up next to him and looked down the sidewalk with him. Once again, I couldn't believe my eyes, but there it was. A four-foot long alligator was running down the sidewalk in the middle courtyard. It wasn't headed our way, but it was probably just a matter of time before it decided to turn in our direction.

Now Mr. Owens had always responded to me with a smile and a "Yes, Mr. Reynolds". I guess I was so used to asking him to do things that I didn't think before I opened my mouth. I don't know why I said it. It just came out.

"Mr. Owens, go get a garbage can and throw it on top of the gator before the kids start coming in." He did not hesitate with his answer.

"No sir. I don't think so." It was the first time Mr. Owens had ever said "no" to me. It was a classic moment. I could see the serious look on his face. I knew my request was most unreasonable and I started laughing at the situation. We kept the children away from the wild creature until the wildlife officer came. He captured it and took it away.

The Chant

At the time, I didn't know the woman yelling at me was Mrs. Lude, Tommy's mother. She was angry because all three of her children had black teachers. Her favorite description of me at the moment was "nigger lover". She yelled it a number of times from her position on the other side of the fence. We didn't have a large number of black teachers in the school and it was just a coincidence her children all had black teachers.

Mrs. Lude was also mad because her younger son, Steven, who was a second grader, told her I had paddled him in my office the day before. I informed her I had only seen Steven one time that week and that was concerning his improper cafeteria behavior. I had never used the paddle on him. I explained that her aggressive nature and verbal abuse would not be tolerated at school and I could have her arrested and banned from the school if she continued her disruptive outbursts.

I was sad for Tommy. On top of all his problems, he had to live with a mother like her. It was almost time for dismissal and I was surprised when Mrs. Lude walked to the main office to sign her children out for the day. Before leaving she demanded her children be given white teachers or she would take her problem to the school board. I decided to respond to her unreasonable demand.

"I'm not changing any teachers on the basis of color." She left with her three interesting children.

Minutes later, I took my post at the school bus loading area next to the library to help direct the traffic. I was recovering from the abuse I had taken from the words of another mentally disturbed parent. How would we be able to help those children if they had to go to a home with such hate and ugly thoughts? Sometimes you just feel lost and helpless. It has been said that if you follow a crazy child home you'll find that a crazy mama opens the door to the house.

In my recovering state, I did not notice I was being watched from the other side of the school fence. I wished I hadn't, but I looked that way when I heard someone call my name. When I turned toward the voice I was greeted by an incredible sight. I couldn't believe my eyes.

Mrs. Lude and her three children, the boy scout from hell, Alvin Lester, a woman I didn't know and a small child were all standing on the outside of the school yard fence. Mrs. Lude was leading the group in a song-type chant.

"Mr. Reynolds is an asshole…asshole…asshole! Say it again, louder! Asshole, asshole!" I had never heard such a cheer. It was well presented and all the participants were in harmony and sync. The only thing missing was the pom-poms. It was ironic, however, that in their insult, they had used "Mister" in front of my name. What a great way to end my day.

I probably should have moved the Lude children to different classes for the sake of the teachers, but I just couldn't allow her to bully us at the school. As usual, the teachers supported my decision, but I'm sure they would have preferred for me to move the troubled children. The aspect of facing that awful mother on a daily basis was too much to ask of any teacher. I should have learned from these and other mistakes, but I was trying to do the right thing.

Both of the Lude boys, Tommy and Steven, were awful during the next two days at school. I was disappointed in Tommy, but we could not allow him or his brother to disrupt the classes. It was obvious their mother had told them to cause all the trouble they could and they did. They were suspended a number of times for fighting with the other students, usually black students, and they were disrespectful to their teachers and any other adult who tried to correct them.

The police caught them one weekend after they had broken into the school. The alarm system alerted our security and they caught the two boys while they were still inside the building vandalizing the classrooms. Both boys were sent to the alternative school as punishment and for extensive counseling. Crystal, the little sister, had a few minor problems in school. She fought with her classmates, too. She was like her mother and quick to call an ugly name. The two brothers would return in twenty days. We would have some relief from our problems with the Ludes, but we had much more coming our way.

Elvis And The Wild Hog

A month after I removed our two P.T.A. ladies from their positions, a husband and wife team, Mr. and Mrs. Adams, volunteered to help us with our P.T.A. They were wonderful and a welcome addition to the school. The couple worked each day to make the educational experience better for the teachers and the students. Our past experiences with parents wanting to help had been disastrous, but we were proud of our new P.T.A. officers. They wanted to have a flea market and cookout to raise money for the school.

We would rent tables and spaces for the locals to display crafts, artwork, garage sale items and what ever they wanted to sell. A neighborhood country-western band with an Elvis impersonator volunteered to entertain during the cookout. It would be free of charge because it would be good practice for him before he and his band went on to play at the local taverns. The band was scheduled to play at the local topless bar.

Our big day arrived. It would be a day for the community to join with the school and perhaps a stronger relationship would be formed. The tables and spaces were full of items for sale, crafts and artwork. The aroma of hot dogs and hamburgers cooking on the grill filled the air. Elvis was alive and well as the crowd gathered to eat, spend a little money for a good cause, sing and dance. It was a great day for a school in the middle of Sin City.   Then came the anticipated and usual "monkey wrench" and once again the community amazed me.

    I really thought my eyes were playing tricks on me when I saw three men in the yard by a trailer next to the school. They hoisted a huge dead hog up into the air and hung the limp beast upside down from a tree limb. Of course, their next action was to begin butchering the monster pig in the clear view of everyone at the flea market. Cutting up a hog put a serious damper on the school fund raising festivities. I'm not sure if it was the invasion of flies or the smell, but we didn't sell many hot dogs that day. Were people crazy, or what?

Clearing the Fence

I gave Mrs. McWilliams the new information after the headache-causing meeting with Sally's half-sister, Betty. Mrs. McWilliams contacted our friendly HRS and a representative went to see Mrs. Dalton again. We were told the organization would investigate the daycare activities, the abuse and the slave-like tactics toward Sally. Betty's story and information would be taken into consideration, but it was all second hand and hearsay at best. There was no record of Betty making reports to HRS concerning Sally. After the meeting with Mrs. Dalton the social worker came to the school and told me a bizarre story about her visit and encounter with the devil woman.

When the social worker Ms. Jones arrived at the house, Ms Dalton would not allow her to enter. Only the threat of police action opened the door and changed Mrs. Dalton's stand. Ms. Jones said she could see that Mrs. Dalton was very nervous. She thought perhaps the woman was nervous because of the investigative visit. When told about the allegations made against her, Mrs. Dalton knew, without being told, her stepdaughter had given the information. She said Betty was always telling lies about her and everyone else, for that matter. She also said Betty had told lies all her life and she was always trying to do something to break up the marriage between Mrs. Dalton and her husband. Betty was crazy jealous of Mrs. Dalton's relationship with her father.

Mrs. Dalton seemed preoccupied as Ms. Jones questioned her and she kept looking out the window at the front of the house. Mrs. Dalton did say she had a few handicapped children staying at her house once in awhile for parents who worked late. She also said Sally was very helpful with the children. Then suddenly, Mrs. Dalton began screaming.

"Get out! Get out! He's comin'!"

Ms. Jones looked out the front window of the house and saw a man coming up the walkway. From the description she had been given she knew it had to be Mr. Dalton. Mrs. Dalton continued to rant and rave.

"He's here, get out!"

Ms. Jones became frightened by Mrs. Dalton's reaction to her husband's arrival. She lost control and followed Mrs. Dalton's hysterical instructions to run. She ran out of the back door of the house and into the fenced-in backyard so Mr. Dalton would not see her. Mrs. Dalton's screaming voice added to Ms. Jones' fear and pushed the social worker beyond her limitations. She ran across the back yard and jumped, dress and heels, trying to clear the chain-linked fence.

In mid-air, Ms. Jones was joined by a young man as he made the same jump. They both hit the ground at the same time. She was even more afraid as she froze there staring at her new unwanted companion. Their eyes met for a split second and he took off again into a wooded area. He was gone.

Ms. Jones realized Mrs. Dalton was not yelling at her. She was yelling at the young man, who must have been hiding somewhere in the house. Ms. Jones could hear the Daltons yelling at each other as she walked to her car. I was, once again, amazed at the adventures around us. We even laughed at the vision of Ms. Jones clearing the fence in her dress and heels. Sometimes you really do have to laugh to keep from crying.

Classic Poem

One of our older and more physically mature fifth graders, Mark, had broken into the car lot of a local dealership and vandalized a large number of the 300ZX model of sports cars. He was arrested late Friday night, released from the youth detention center on Saturday afternoon and he was back in school on Monday morning. He was the school's hero for the week. The students talked about him like he was our number one scholar. He walked around school like he was a rooster in a hen house.

I wasn't sure how to keep our students from considering the criminal elements of the area worthy of praise. How could we combat the glory given to students like Mark who caused such problems in the neighborhood. It would always be difficult for us because we only had them about seven hours of the day and then they went home. Teachers were frustrated because if the student took a step forward academically or socially while they were with us, they would take two steps backward when they were away from us. In most cases the teachers had to start over from step one each day. I had just finished the morning announcements when our office secretary, Mrs. Highsmith, told me I needed to answer a call from a parent; an angry parent.

"Good morning, this is Bill Reynolds, may I help you?" The man on the other end of the phone line did not introduce himself.

"I'm keepin' my daughter home until the school stops teachin' that nasty crap. What's the hell's goin' on up there?"

"Sir, I'm not sure what has happened to upset you. Tell me who you are and what's wrong. I'll try to help."

"It don't matter who I am. She ain't learnin' them nasty poems. And you better not fail her if she don't learn that poem. I can't believe ya'll teach this crap."

"Sir, I don't think we'll ever fail a child over a poem. If you don't want her to learn it she doesn't have to. Can you tell me why the poem offends you?"

"Hell yes, I can tell ya. It's that pussy poem."

"Excuse me, sir. What pussy poem?"

"Here, dammit, I'll read it to ya. The owl and the pussy cat went to sea…"

"Sir, please let me interrupt you for a moment. That poem is a well-known children's classic. Students learn that poem all the time."

"Wait, you didn't let me finish. Just listen to this part…. Oh pussy, oh pussy, my beautiful pussy…. Now, my daughter ain't learnin' 'bout no pussy, she ain't talkin' 'bout no pussy, and she damn sure ain't givin' up no pussy. And you and that school of yours can kiss my ass." Sometimes ignorance is truly overwhelming. Were people crazy, or what?

Insanity

I wasn't sure what actions, if any, were being initiated by the HRS, but I knew Sally Dalton was as sad and distant as she had ever been. She was doing very little schoolwork, she talked to no one, and it seemed to me that her eyes grew even older. Sally had been tested for our gifted program, so she was more than capable when it came to her schoolwork. I personally tried not to think about Sally's situation for a few days, but thank goodness for Mrs. McWilliams. As usual, she brought me back to my senses.

"Mr. Reynolds, we can not stand by and allow this intelligent, beautiful child to be destroyed by her insane parents. It's happening right before our eyes."

Talk about a reality check, Mrs. McWilliams gave me a big one. We decided Mrs. McWilliams would try to talk to Sally each day, in order to gain her trust and once again give her someone to look to for help. During their second day of talks, Sally told Mrs. McWilliams about the babysitter, Jimmy. Sally's story wasn't something we could ignore.

Jimmy and her mother liked to wrestle on the floor. Sometimes Sally would play too. Sally didn't like Jimmy very much anymore because when her mother was gone, he made Sally take all her clothes off and told her to go hide. He wanted to find her. One time she hid under the bed, but when he found her he pulled her out from under the bed by her feet. Jimmy threw her up on the bed and then lay on top of her. She couldn't breathe.

Another time, when she heard her parents leave, she ran and hid in the closet before Jimmy could get her. She thought she was safe, but after a little while he came to the door of the closet and scared her. He scratched on the door and whispered, "Saaaally, I'm gonna get you."

Sally said it scared her so bad she wet her pants and thought she was going to throw up in the closet. Later that night, Jimmy chased her around and they were both naked. We called the HRS, the police and the school security. Then we called Mr. Dalton. He had told me he wanted to know when we heard something from Sally. He seemed concerned about the information I gave him. When I told him I was calling the police and HRS he said, "If what you say is true, you won't have to call anyone else. I'll take care of him myself."

I wanted to tell him I had already heard about how he took care of problems, but it was just a passing thought. Mr. Dalton told me his wife would be gone for a few days and Jimmy would not be at the house at all. Sally would be safe there with him. She could stay in school for the rest of the day and he would pick her up when school was out. I didn't have any problems with what he wanted to do because I was going to call the police anyway.

The police arrived before the HRS worker and after hearing the story, went to visit Mr. Dalton's garage. About two hours later an HRS worker came to assist us. She was replacing the previous worker and didn't know much about Sally's case and background. We knew we couldn't tell her about all the problems we were having with the Daltons, but we could relate Sally's new story about Jimmy. It was disappointing that the worker wasn't familiar with Sally's situation. She did, with Mrs. McWilliams' urging, decide to take Sally with her.

As they were leaving a police officer returned to school from his visit with Mr. Dalton. He talked to the HRS worker and they both went to see Mr. Dalton again. We were never told what went on at the meeting, but I do know Sally stayed at home with her father that night.

The next morning I was ready to follow up on the situation with Sally. If the HRS worker had not done something by day's end, I planned to contact other authorities for help. It didn't take very long that morning for more fuel to be added to the fire.

I was caught completely off guard when Mr. Dalton, the devil woman, and Jimmy, the babysitter from hell, all walked into my office. It was the first time I had seen Jimmy up close and in person. He had sandy blond hair, cut short and actually, he was not a bad looking man. I could tell he was a country boy. He had that look. He was taller than me, but that was not saying much. I was thicker. The three of them were masters of intimidation. They moved into my office like a small pack of wild dogs and they intended to make me their next victim. Some people, if I should call them people, actually thrive on the fear of others. I felt trapped and alone in my office. They were accomplishing what they wanted. I was scared. I tried not to show it, but I'm sure they knew. Dogs can always sense the fear in their prey. The principal of an elementary school should never have to face such fear nor feelings. Educating children is supposed to be fun and rewarding.

The evil trio was draining me of my sense of reason and there was no doubt their goal was my demise. I had not seen Mrs. Dalton since I heard the rumors she started about me. As usual, she was the first aggressor as she closed my office door.

"I don't think you know what you're doin' here, shithead. You're gonna get hurt and you're too stupid to see it." I saw Mrs. McWilliams through the small window of the door. I knew she had recognized the stressful look on my face and she would call the police. The scare tactics began.

"You ain't gonna come here and try to run my family. My family ain't none of your business." I wanted to say something without my voice quivering. I raised my hand and pointed at Jimmy.

"When you allow this creep to hurt Sally, it becomes my business." Jimmy's eyes widened and he stepped toward me. I stood up and stepped to meet him. He stopped and I could tell he was surprised I had moved with him. We stared at each other as Mrs. Dalton added her sarcasm to the tense moment.

"Be careful, Jimmy, he'll hit you with a bat." Jimmy's courage was building and I knew I would soon have to make a decision about defending myself. The door to my office opened and my salvation came in the voice of Mrs. McWilliams.

"Mr. Reynolds, the police are on their way. Are you all right?" Did I love Mrs. McWilliams or what?

I watched Jimmy. He was the closest one to me. It was easy to see none of them liked the idea of the police headed our way. I personally wished they had come with sirens blaring so we could hear them from a distance. That always has a great effect in the movies. The room was silent for a moment, but Mrs. Dalton still wanted to attack and intimidate.

"This ain't over yet, asshole. Just keep bein' stupid."

Mr. Dalton had not said a word during the verbal confrontation. All four were standing in front of me, including Sally. I wanted to keep Sally with me at school, but I knew only the police would be able to do that and they were still on their way. Once again I was amazed as Mrs. Dalton put her fat arm around Sally.

"You go on to class, honey. You gotta get your education." I really hated that woman. Mrs. McWilliams stood at the door.

"Here Sally, I'll get you a late slip for class." Sally walked with Mrs. McWilliams as the evil trio moved toward the door. Jimmy was the last to leave the office and with a half smile he made a stand as he whispered back to me.

"You're mine, boy. Get ready." He followed the others out of the office.

After his threat I took a moment to slow my heart beat and then stepped into the main office area to be sure they were gone. It was easy for me to see the concerned looks on the faces of the staff, so I assured them I was all right. I was just tired of the insanity.

The police arrived after the Daltons were gone. Again, I had to explain the Sally situation to the officer. I told him of the threats and intimidation, but I knew verbal threats had little substance as a crime. The police officer went to talk to the Daltons.

After the officer left, Mrs. McWilliams called the HRS, but they could not send anyone until later in the day. Just before school was dismissed that day I received a call from one of the social workers that had dealt with the Daltons before. It was good to talk to someone knowledgeable of the Daltons. The social worker had already made arrangements to meet with the Daltons the following day. Her schedule was full at that time, but she assured me the meeting would change Sally's situation.

Mrs. McWilliams and I stood at the front of the school while the children were being dismissed. Sally was standing on the sidewalk, waiting on her father to pick her up. I was glad the day was over and I didn't think Sally's sad life would end with the big meeting with HRS the next day. Then my heart was broken again as a white Volkswagen pulled up to the curb where Sally was standing. Sally got into the little car and I was shocked when I realized that Jimmy was at the wheel. He smiled at me and waved as he drove away. I couldn't believe her parents had allowed that awful man to pick her up. I was sick to my stomach and all I wanted to do was go home and see that my own daughter was safe and tell her how much I loved her.

After most of the students had gone home I went back into my office. It was going to be difficult not to take the events of the day home with me. I really didn't want to. I wanted to leave it all in Sin City. I realized how nervous it all had made me when I jumped at the sound of the phone ringing. I picked it up as usual, but I was sorry I did.

"This is Bill Reynolds." My blood went cold when I heard the voice at the other end of the line.

"Hey, shithead." I recognized Jimmy's voice. "I'll kiss Sally good night for ya." The phone went dead. I didn't want to think it was true, but I was more than capable of killing him at that moment. I had no idea how I would be able to survive the awful challenge before me. Was this a new level of insanity, or what?

The Wacker

Everybody picked on David. He acted silly all the time and the other students just couldn't help it. I'm sure if I had been a fellow student, I would have picked on him, too. He was one of those children who were tailor-made for teasing. We have all seen someone like David during our lives. He made it almost impossible for the other students to leave him alone.

His appearance didn't help the situation. David was very over-weight and he was a victim of the parental head lice philosophy of, "shave their heads so we can see the damn things". He wore eyeglasses with big thick circular lenses that magnified his eyes far beyond their true size. His rotund appearance and his silly actions made him a perfect target for ridiculing from his peers.

I met his mother and she told me how she had been teased when she was in school. She had bug-eyes without the thick glasses. I had no doubt she was telling the truth. She could not accept the thought that David brought his many problems on himself. She let me know it was the school's responsibility to stop the hazing from happening.

To make David's problems even worse, his personal hygiene was very poor. He was dirty and had an odor, to put it mildly. Once again, our teachers and staff did all they could to help David. We talked to his classmates, asked his mother to stop shaving his head, and kept deodorant on hand for him. The teachers went far beyond the call of their educational responsibilities. Good teachers always do that for their students. Our efforts seemed to be working and his mother was pleased with the outcome. She came to the school and stood and watched David eat breakfast each morning in the cafeteria. Her presence in the morning also helped deter the students who would have teased him if she were not watching.

Then came the morning I will never forget as long as I live. To this day and forever, I will never know why I was so stupid. It was Monday morning and the early students were arriving a few at a time. I heard a voice behind me on the sidewalk outside my office. As the person came closer, I recognized that it was David's mother and she was mad about something. It was too early in the day or the week for her to be that mad. She didn't stop at the front desk, but walked directly into my office. David was in tow. I wanted to hurry, close the door and hide in my closet-like bathroom, but she was too fast and she was on me like a tiger.

"I've had it with this school. This is the last time. I'm not puttin' up with this anymore." I heard what she was saying, but I was more interested and amazed at her appearance. She must have just rolled out of bed and walked over to yell at me. She wore a stained, once white, smock like dress. It might have been a nightgown. She had bare feet; dirty bare feet, dirty bare feet with cracks in them. Her hair was uncombed with one side sticking straight up into the air. The other side was matted to the side of her head. Along with her horrifying morning appearance she brought her morning breath. No commercial on television could have done justice to that moment in my office. There were not enough Tic-Tacs in the world to calm the dragon behind her breath. It was a halitosis nightmare classic and I was the victim. I had to interrupt the one sided conversation.

"Please stop yelling. What could I have done to you this early? What has happened?" She was ready.

"It happened last Friday after school. I was late getting here to pick up David, so he started walkin' home. Some big boy from another school beat him up near the apartments."

Now, before I continue to tell this story, please think about what she said to me and why she was so mad. The problem happened after school on Friday of the last week. She was in my office on Monday. A boy from another school near where they lived had beaten up David and she was mad at me. Were people crazy, or what? She had more for me.

"You said you would help us and he would be safe. You lied to me." I had to comment on the verbal berating.

"I have no control over what happens in your apartment complex. I'm sorry he walked home, but you were late and I think you're more upset with yourself. You should have called the police if someone hurt him."

She began crying and sobbing, which added greatly to her morning glory. She looked bad enough without the tears. I didn't know how much longer I could stay in the office with her. I was becoming nauseous and fading fast. She talked and blubbered at the same time.

"I can't take anymore of this. Nobody helps us. David is so strange, nobody likes him and he acts so stupid all the time. He has no father and yes, I do know how silly he is at school."

I looked at David. He made a silly face and moved his eyebrows up and down. I wanted to slap him out of the chair. The thought flashed through my head, but it remained only a thought. Even though I was pressed with the situation and nauseated by her appearance and lack of hygiene, I still felt sad for the wretched creature and wanted to help. She was on the edge. We could not allow our hearts to become hard and uncaring. Education is a caring business. We were professionals. At that moment of weakness another unbelievable adventure began for me with her pathetic words.

"I'm so sorry, Mr. Reynolds, that I talked so ugly to you. I know it's not your fault. You have been good to David. I'm really sorry about all this. I just don't know what to do. I don't know what will become of David. What kind'a man will he be? He is my son and I love him." She was pitiful. I was jell-o and a real fish at that moment. She had more to share.

"David really got hurt. He got kicked in his "privates" and it's real bad. I think he needs to see a doctor, but I don't have any insurance and no way to get to the free clinic. If you could just take a look at him, you could tell me if you think it's bad or not and what I should do."

Again, I didn't want to hear what she had to say. I looked at David again. He smiled and his eyebrows went up and down once more. I wanted to kick him in his privates myself. He was really annoying and downright, "goofy". I had no desire to inspect his privates. I thought maybe, if I didn't respond, it might go away. It could have been a bad dream. She was, however, quick to bring me back to the reality of my office.

"Men know more about these things. Please just take a look and tell me what you think." I'm still not sure why, but I took a deep breath; well, not a deep one. She was still near me. I then ran this rationale through my head.

"He is just a little boy. His mother is here and it is her request. I may be able to tell her something about the injury. She really needs someone to step forward and help her. We can use my little closet-like bathroom for his privacy and I can handle this adult situation professionally." I am still haunted by the vision of the three of us standing in that bathroom. I should have had another staff member with us, but I don't know where I would have put them. Besides, I was too embarrassed to ask anyone to join us. I realized right away, as the three of us stood there, my soft heart had really overloaded my sensibilities and put me in what could have been a serious situation. I was getting ready to give a testicle exam while mother watched wearing what I really think was her nightgown. David stood in the corner of the small room. I was in the middle and mother was at the door. She kept the nightmare going.

"Pull your pants down, son, and show Mr. Reynolds." I don't know if I went dizzy from her odor or her request. Either way, I was light-headed. David did not hesitate. In fact, he seemed quite eager to expose himself. Down went his pants. He wore no underwear, making his exposure instant. I looked down and saw no injury at all. No marks, no bruises, he looked normal.

"I don't see a problem here. He looks fine to me. Does it hurt?" David nodded his head, "yes". "Well, I don't see anything wrong." The adventure moved along. She made sure of that.

"You can't just see it. It's underneath his little wacker. Lift it up, you'll see it."

Now the words, "Lift it up, you'll see it", hit me like a ton of bricks. I thought perhaps I was dreaming or the fumes had finally gotten to me and I was delirious. Even if I could see it, I wasn't going to lift it up. I tried to come to my senses.

"David, you lift it up and I'll take a look." Mother was quick to join in.

"He won't touch it. He has a thing about touchin' it. We think it's because the babysitter he had one time sucked on it and he ain't touched it since. I even have to hold it sometimes when he pees and I have to keep it clean. I hope he comes out of this before he gets older."

It had become a classic adventure in every sense of the word. I was caught up in the craziness. I turned toward David, lifted it up and took a look. He had a large blood filled blister of some kind on his testicle sack. It looked bad and he did need medical attention. I put it down and lifted my head looking into David's eyes. He smiled that goofy smile and his eyebrows moved up and down, adding to my discomfort. I told the mother she needed to seek medical attention for David. I scrubbed a layer of skin off my hands as I washed them in the sink. Was I crazy, or what?

What's The Charge?

That night I attended a high school basketball game and ran into an old friend, Ralph Moneyhun. He was a detective with the sheriff's department and as we talked about old times, the problems I had been having with the Daltons came to my mind. I didn't like taking my work home with me, but I thought Ralph could give me some advice. I didn't want to take his mind off of the fun he was having that evening so I asked him to meet with me one day soon. He was a good man. He came to see me at school the very next day.

It took me about an hour to tell him all the events that had occurred in my dealings with the Daltons. I'm sure, as a detective, he had seen and heard other stories about abused children. I could tell he was at a state in his career where nothing surprised or shocked him. I was getting that way myself. He wanted to help and would get back with me later to discuss our next step.

After Detective Moneyhun left, Mrs. McWilliams came to my office with Sally. The child had been beaten the night before and she had belt marks on her arms, neck, back and legs. Mrs. McWilliams was outraged.

"How many times do we have to send this baby back to that house?" She was right again. It had to stop. I called Ralph and told him. He was on his way back to school to see the child. It wasn't long before he was back in my office examining Sally's injuries. It was as if Mrs. Dalton was once again challenging us to do something about it. Detective Moneyhun thought the same thing. It was her form of defiance and intimidation. She did not care about the possible consequences for her abuse, or perhaps, she really didn't think there would be any consequences at all. The awful woman thought she was untouchable and actually, up to that point, she had been.

Detective Moneyhun made two phone calls from my office. Within minutes, an evidence technician was taking pictures of the marks on Sally's body while six police officers stood in my office discussing the arrest of the Daltons. Then, Ralph decided what we would do.

"Bill, what will they do if you call them and tell them you are turning Sally over to HRS?" I knew exactly what would happen. I pointed to my office window.

"As crazy and aggressive as they have been lately, I think they will drive around that corner in their truck and come to get Sally. I'm sure they'll come here first, ready to fight." My friend, Detective Moneyhun was ready to stop the Daltons' abuse.

"Call 'em." He directed his officers as I made the call. Mrs. Dalton answered.

"This is Mr. Reynolds. I'm taking Sally to the hospital because of the marks on her and then I'm turning her over to HRS. I just thought you needed to know that." She yelled one statement and hung up.

"That's it. You're dead."

I was instructed to stand at the front counter in the main office. The officers were stationed in different areas of the office area, but out of sight. The marked patrol cars were moved from the front of the school. Within five minutes, after my brief conversation with Mrs. Dalton, the truck drove around the corner just as I had predicted. The truck pulled up to the front of the school and both Daltons jumped out. My heart raced out of control as they slammed through the front door and rushed toward the counter, where I was standing. Mrs. Dalton was, as usual, the first to attack.

"You son-of-a-bitch. Where's Sally?"

I stepped back as Mr. Dalton reached across the counter to grab me. At that moment, Detective Moneyhun and his officers came to my rescue from all sides. Both Mr. and Mrs. Dalton were physically taken down to the floor in one continuous motion. It was just like watching a movie. I couldn't believe it was happening at school. They were both on the floor with guns to their heads. One officer read them their rights and told them they were under arrest for child abuse, disturbing the peace, disrupting the educational process of a school and a few other things I don't remember. It was exciting and Mrs. Dalton wasn't disappointing, as she amazed me one more time. With her face against the floor, she was still defiant as one of the officers handcuffed her.

"What's the charge, again?" She was crazy and she was going to jail.

Detective Moneyhun made one more phone call before he left and told me to expect to hear from the State Attorney's office. It would be a Ms. Watt and I would probably have to meet with her about the Daltons.

The school office staff was in shock over the wild events of the morning and they were trying to explain what had taken place to the other members of the faculty and staff. There was no way to re-create what actually happened. It was one of those times when you just had to be there.

Sally's stepsister, Betty, made arrangements with the HRS to allow her to take Sally home with her that night. About two o'clock that day, I received another strange phone call. It was Charlie, the big man Mrs. Dalton had brought to school to hurt me the day I pulled out the baseball bat.

"Is this Mr. Reynolds?"

"Yes, may I help you?"

"This is Charlie, Mrs. Dalton's friend. I have an emergency here. Is she still at school with you?"

"No, she's gone."

"When did she leave? Is she on her way home?"

"I don't think so. She was arrested."

"Oh, that's just great! Now, I'm stuck with all these creepy kids. These kids got them shunts in their heads."

"Shunts? I don't know what you mean." We were talking like we were old friends, even though he was going to break my legs.

"You know, them things these kind'a kids got to keep their heads up. Those shunts on their heads. Somebody's gotta come get these kids. I can't stay here. I'm late for work already. Besides these kids give me the willies." I knew some children were not in a very good situation and I also knew I had to do something about it. My job is to take care of the children.

"Charlie, just stay there for a little while longer and I'll send someone to help you." He was frustrated and I'm sure, mentally disturbed.

"Okay man, but I ain't got nothin' to do with this crazy stuff. It ain't my fault. I just want out of here." I hung up, called Detective Moneyhun and gave him the crazy information. He was sending a patrol car to the Dalton house. I was too involved and curious, so I went to see what was going on myself. I couldn't help it. I was glad I arrived the same time the police did. It was the same officer who earlier, had taken Mrs. Dalton to the floor in the office at school. Charlie was gone, but we found six children, each with a different physical handicap. Three were in wheelchairs, two in braces and one with physical limitations, but no apparatus needed. Two of the children in wheelchairs needed neck braces to keep their heads straight and upright. I guess that's what Charlie meant when he said they had shunts in their heads. During the next two weeks following the Dalton's arrest, the events were non-stop.

Mrs. Dalton was charged with a number of crimes and held without bond. I had to appear at a bond hearing and testify against her so the judge would not allow her out on bail. Mr. Dalton was released and Jimmy, the abusive babysitter, left town. Charlie was gone too. People like that are always ready to run. Betty, the stepsister, was given custody of Sally. I'm not sure why, but Sally's handicapped brother stayed with Mr. Dalton. Mr. Dalton lost his job as a county school bus driver and the Dalton daycare from hell for handicapped children, was no longer in operation. Mr. Dalton called me at school and let me know I would pay for the problems I had caused his family.

Mrs. McWilliams and I met with Ms. Watts, the State Attorney, and told her of our long and sad battle with the abusive Daltons. I was receiving threatening phone calls on a daily basis. Most of the time the caller would tell me not to testify against Mrs. Dalton if there was a trial. The devil woman's intimidation tactics even reached out from her jail cell.

Sally's sister, Betty, met with Detective Moneyhun at my office and told him she heard that her father had hired someone to hurt me or even kill me. She said he had done such things before. She refused to tell Ralph about the past and only warned us about the possibilities. Ralph met with the school security, and with the county superintendent's permission, Pinkerton security guards were hired to protect me at school. They were to stay with me until I went to testify against Mrs. Dalton.

The two guards they sent to the school seemed like little boys. I was afraid that if someone did come to school to harm me, I would have to protect the young men and myself, even though they had been sent to protect me. I had my doubts about their abilities as bodyguards, but I'm sure they had good intentions as they followed me around the campus. Fortunately, the two young men did not have to use their skills to protect me.

A week later, I sat in the county courthouse and told the bizarre stories surrounding Sally's life with the devil woman. She was sentenced to one year in jail and she would not be allowed to see Sally until the child turned eighteen years old. Then Sally would be able to make her own mind up about seeing her mother. Mrs. McWilliams received the most wonderful letter from the State Attorney's office commending us on our efforts on Sally's behalf. Sally continued to attend school under Betty's supervision. From then on, the child was clean, well dressed and seemed happy.

Two weeks after Mrs. Dalton was sent to jail, Detective Moneyhun called me at school early one morning. He asked me if I was sitting down, because he had a story to tell me and he wanted to be sure I was sitting down before he told me. Needless to say, I was extremely curious and assured him I was sitting down. He told me this story.

When Mrs. Dalton was nineteen years old she lived in South Carolina. Her own father put nude pictures of her in one of those male porn magazines. Under the picture was this caption:

" $25,000 to the first man who will come to South Carolina and marry this woman."

Mr. Dalton read the ad, made the trip to South Carolina, married the devil woman, collected the money and returned with his evil and mentally disturbed new bride. Were people crazy, or what?

A Bad Picture

When Mrs. Biggs sent Jamie running to my office, I knew something was very wrong. Mrs. Biggs never needed help in her classroom. Good teachers usually take care of most of their own classroom problems. If she was calling for me she really needed help.

"Mr. Reynolds, come quick! William is really being bad and Mrs. Biggs needs you to come." I hurried to the fourth grade wing. Mrs. Biggs met me at the door and it was obvious she was stressed to her limits.

"Mr. Reynolds, William is very angry about something and he is being very disrespectful to me and his classmates. He refused to leave the room when I told him to go to your office." I walked over to where William was sitting in his desk. He was looking down and his breathing was heavy and dramatic. William was a handsome black child with high cheekbones and black eyes. He was larger than most fourth graders.

"William, please stand up and walk with me like a gentleman to my office." He stood up quickly and pushed the desk over on its side. I reached down to stop his aggressive behavior, but that was his final act of defiance and he did not continue. I made him pick the desk up then I took his arm. We left the classroom and headed to my office. As we walked, William attempted to pull away from me, but there was nothing really major. I was able to control him and keep us moving toward the office. His heavy breathing continued as we walked. I wasn't sure if he could control that or not. It was a little too dramatic to be real, but perhaps it was. When we finally reached the office he tried to pull away again, but I knew that was just for the benefit of the office staff.

We walked into my office and William threw himself into one of the chairs and began rocking back and forth, hitting his head on the back of the chair. I asked him to "please stop", but be ignored me. I asked Mrs. McWilliams to join us. I knew she would have a calming affect on a student like William. In fact, she kept all of us calm. Perhaps I needed her there to keep me in the professional mode that was required from the principal. She sat with us and talked to William as I spoke on the telephone. It was the first time I had ever spoken to William's mother. She seemed very pleasant and concerned. She said she was leaving work and would meet us in fifteen minutes.

While we waited, Mrs. McWilliams informed me she had been working with William on controlling his temper at school and she thought he had been doing very well until his behavior that day. She was surprised and disappointed, because she was hoping he was improving. She wanted me to know more about him.

"William never gives us any reasons for his outbursts. He never seems to know why he gets so mad."

William didn't change his expression as she talked, but he did continue to overemphasize his breathing. His mother walked into my office and a new adventure in my life as the principal began. I would later wish I had taken the day off.

Mrs. Jones was very attractive and well dressed. William had her facial features and skin tone. He was still breathing heavily when his mother sat down next to him. She looked at her son.

"Why are you doing that? Stop breathing like that."

Mrs. Jones was calm and we were all waiting for William to answer his mother's question and demand. No answer came and his breathing became even more dramatic. I could see Mrs. Jones was embarrassed by her son's lack of respect for everyone in the room, including her.

"You better stop that silly breathing and talk to me. It makes these people think you're crazy or something. Now, stop and tell me why you're acting like this. What's wrong?" William made no response. He glared straight ahead and continued his heavy breathing. "Mr. Reynolds, I'm going to take William home and I assure you when he returns to school, he will be a different young man. Please tell Mrs. Biggs I am so sorry."

I appreciated her thoughts, but I didn't believe it would be that easy. She stood up and reached for William's arm. The moment she touched him, he went absolutely wild. I had never seen anything like it before. It took us all by surprise.

William pushed her violently as he jumped to his feet. He grabbed her necklace and tore it from her neck. The small fake pearl beads bounced on the floor and rolled all over the office. She tried to grab him and he hit her in the face with a closed fist. It was not a child's hit or slap. It was a full-grown man's blow to her face. The disbelief on her face was only matched by the horror on mine. We were all in a state of shock.

Once again, I couldn't believe my eyes as he ripped her blouse, popping off most of the buttons, causing it to burst open and expose her bra. She struggled to keep her blouse from being torn completely off as he continued to pull at her. She moved away from him and tried to cover herself. He took advantage of the moment and kicked her in the leg before I could reach him and assist her. I took William to the floor and held him there against the carpet. Mrs. McWilliams went to help William's battered and crying mother.

It was obvious that the kick to her leg really hurt her. William tried to bite me as I held him on the floor. It was hard to hold him without hurting him. He began to rub his head on the carpeted floor, leaving a scratch like rug burn on the skin of his forehead. He was much stronger than his small, ten-year-old body looked to be. It was difficult for me to hold him. I knew his mother was in a state of shock from his aggression and also from the beating she had taken. Mrs. McWilliams tried to help her pull herself together. Mrs. Gilmer and Mrs. Frye, two other members of the staff, joined us. Along with Mrs. McWilliams, we were able to hold William without hurting him or his injuring anyone else.

Mrs. Jones asked us to help get William to her car so she could take him home. She would get in touch with his father and have him meet them at the doctor's office. She was drained, confused and visibly shaken both mentally and physically by her son's actions. I really felt bad for her, but I had no answer or solution for the situation. I was glad she was there to take him home. We would deal with the school disturbance later and follow our procedures for such serious and disruptive action. For the moment, however, we needed to settle and re-group. Mrs. Jones was in tears.

"Mr. Reynolds, I have no explanation for his awful behavior." I didn't want her to worry about us. She needed to get William some help.

"Let's just get him home. We'll talk after all this settles down."

Mrs. Jones asked us to release William and she promised he would not fight anymore. We had our doubts, but we cautiously allowed him to stand up. He looked tired and still angry. We were all tired and angry. He did not fight as he and his mother stared at each other. Mother broke the stare.

"Let's go." She did not touch him and he knew she was disgusted and ashamed of the unpleasant encounter. I accompanied them as they walked out into the main office. I wanted to hold William because I thought he would run when they walked outside. William was between his mother and me as we walked out of the building toward the parking lot. As we approached the car Mrs. Jones took William by his arm again. She must have had doubts about him getting into the car. I didn't see it, but he must have given her some resistance as we walked.

"If you don't stop this, I am going to knock your eyeballs out of your head." She jerked his arm. "Now, stop and get in that car."

He tried to pull away from her, but she picked him up and started moving toward the car. He began his violent swinging and kicking again. I grabbed his legs. She had his upper body. Together we were able to carry him to the car.

Again, his strength was amazing for a child his age and size. He was very strong and hard to hold. Mrs. Jones opened the car door, but getting William into the car was a different story. We just couldn't do it. We would have really had to hurt him to get him into that car. If we released him he was going to run and if we held him, we would have to fight. Someone was going to get hurt.

Mrs. Jones' frustration and embarrassment level finally over-whelmed her and she, like William, went wild, matching kick for kick and blow for blow. She pushed and hit William, beating him into the front seat of the car. He kicked the dashboard, caving in the door of the glove compartment. Mrs. Jones got into the car with him and started tearing off his clothes. I was standing there watching it all happen and I couldn't believe my eyes. He screamed and fought back as she pulled and ripped his shirt. Then she pulled off his pants. He was trapped in the front seat and Mrs. Jones took advantage of her sudden advantage over William. She continued to beat him and rip off his clothes. I watched in amazement as she actually tore off his underwear. When she stopped, William had one tennis shoe on one foot. She was exhausted.

"See if you run now, boy." She had made her stand and she was in control for the first time. It was a control she wanted to strengthen even more. The misadventure continued and intensified when she grabbed the shoulder strap of the seatbelt and wrapped it around William's neck and head, holding it with her right hand. William could not move because he was actually tied up. I couldn't move because I was frozen with disbelief. Her new chokehold and William's fear stopped all of his wild actions and movement. If he flinched she pulled the strap tighter. She held the strap as she turned the key in the ignition with her left hand. As the car started, the bizarre encounter escalated to a new level of insanity.

William kicked his foot up in her direction. The lone tennis shoe landed full force on the point of her chin. It was another huge blow to her already battered face. Her eyes rolled back in her head and she fell across the steering wheel, sounding the horn. I knew she was unconscious the moment her head hit the horn. I reached through the opened window and lifted her head off the steering wheel, stopping the sound of the horn. William took the moment to unwrap the strap from his neck and he jumped out of the car. He was naked except for the one shoe. He ran and stood behind another car as if he wanted to be free, but hidden because of his nakedness. Mrs. Jones made noises as she regained her consciousness. She was injured and dazed from the kick. Mrs. McWilliams came to help me and she continued the efforts to revive Mrs. Jones.

I went after William, but he was not an easy catch. He dodged in and out of parked cars, all the time trying to stay hidden as well as to get away. It was obvious he didn't want to be seen in his naked state. The only restriction he had was the fence surrounding the teacher's parking lot. I finally managed to catch him in the corner of the parking lot as he tried to climb the fence. I pulled him down and we struggled again, as I carried him back to the car. I wasn't proud of the sight I had created for the neighborhood to witness. There was the principal of the school, chasing and capturing a completely naked child, and then carrying him, kicking and fighting, back to a car, where the child's angry and semi-conscious mother was waiting with a seat belt noose. Something was bad, bad wrong with that picture. I knew it had gotten out of hand as I walked through the parking lot, carrying a tired, naked, mentally disturbed child. I knew it would be in the "top ten" list of how "not" to handle a situation. I was never taught about such encounters in the educational courses I took in collage. I knew I would have to make better decisions from that point on. I just had to get through that present dilemma.

I leaned William against the back of the car. We were both sweating like pigs, especially me. Mrs. McWilliams brought William's pants to him. He quickly put them on while I held on to him. I was not going to release him again. Mrs. Jones stepped out of the car and moved toward us. I cannot describe the look on her battered face. I was afraid I would not be able to control William and his mother if they started fighting again. Then, as usual, Mrs. McWilliams saved me.

"Mr. Reynolds, this is crazy. I'm calling the police and let them take care of this." She was right. I moved William away from his mother. Mrs. McWilliams took Mrs. Jones into the school to attend to her injuries and help her clean up. I held William until the police arrived.

After I explained what had happened to the police, the battle with William raged once again as they tried to put him into the patrol car. He had to be handcuffed and they even had to tie his legs. The sight of that little ten-year-old lying face down in the back seat of a police car made me sick to my stomach. He was actually hog-tied and it looked awful. William was released to the custody of his father later that day.

Two days later William's parents filed a complaint against me for abusing their son. I was questioned by HRS about the marks on William's forehead. William had said I hit him in the head with my fist during the confrontation. After talking with me the HRS reported the charges as being unfounded, but I was still upset about being questioned as the possible abuser. I thought about a new line of work. It just didn't seem worth the effort. William's father called the school and told me he would put marks on my head if he ever saw me again.

Mrs. McWilliams found out, some time later, that medical tests were conducted on William after a similar violent explosion at another school. He had been put on medication for a chemical imbalance and seizures. Were people crazy, or what?

The Devil Woman Is Free

Mrs. Dalton had been in jail for four months when I received an interesting phone call from Ms. Watts, the State Attorney. She informed me that Mrs. Dalton was being released from jail and she would be going home within the week. Part of her probation was to stay away from the school. I couldn't believe she had only spent four months as a punishment for her abuse. Sally finished the next two months with us at school and summer arrived.

In July of that summer, Ms. Watts called me again. She told me a judge in town had given Sally back to her mother and I was not to interfere with the reunion of the Dalton family. She also said in many cases, the courts try to keep the family units together. I was extremely angry and frustrated, and once again sick to my stomach. Sally was given a special assignment to attend another school in the area at her parent's request. I felt as if our efforts to protect Sally meant nothing. I was sure the judge who made the decision to give Sally back to her mother knew nothing about the case. I asked Ms. Watts what we could do, but she said it was over and out of my hands. Actually it was none of my business. I told Ms. Watts that when Sally died at the hands of her crazy mother, I would sue the system in Sally's name.

Ms. Watts was kind and understood my frustration, but we were all bound by the court ruling. We heard nothing about Sally and her family for quite awhile. Her father was no longer driving the school bus for the county. We did hear Ms. Dalton was babysitting for some of the area residents. I did not get involved again.

Each day that week, I had seen a young man named Richard in my office for his improper behavior in class. If I had known at the time Richard was going to lead me into such a dangerous situation, I would have never made the phone call to his mother. The parental contact initiated this hair-raising adventure.

After I explained the week we had with Richard, his mother assured me he would change and be better the next week. The first thing parents do is make that assurance. We didn't hear much from Richard for the next few days at school, but there was talk about him in the streets. The students had all the information. Richard had been picked up for shoplifting in a local department store. After being out of school for a few days, he returned to school and continued his disruptive behavior in the classrooms and around the school campus in general. He caused trouble wherever he was. I was sure his mother had not talked to him at all.

I suspended Richard from school and he could not return until his mother met with me. His mother and stepfather came to school with Richard the next day. His mother never said one word during our meeting, but her husband had plenty to say. Much more than I wanted or needed to hear.

He was a Mexican-American, with the body of a professional wrestler. His face was hard and pitted by acne scars from a bad complexion. He was very muscular and his appearance was the epitome of intimidation at the highest level. He was aggressive in his speech and mannerisms. His appearance was scary enough without his aggressive tone. He wore a sleeveless tank top shirt, which exposed his huge arms and massive, muscular chest. I guess if you were built like that, there are rules about wearing clothes that show off your body. By my standards, he was also extremely ugly. But what did I know? I was just scared.

"We gotta get this shit settled, right now." My heart raced in my much smaller chest as he continued. "Richard says y'all are pickin' on him all the time 'cause he's mix blooded. I want it stopped."

I didn't want to show any fear, but I'm sure he knew. People like him always know. They live to scare people. "Sir, Richard is very disrespectful to the teachers and every adult he comes in contact with. We need your help."

"Get off his back. That will help."

"We don't start out looking for Richard to misbehave. He's easy to find because he creates problems. He does it on his own."

"Well, I don't want you to call my wife no more and I don't want him suspended. Do you hear me?" He spoke to me like I was the child.

"I hear you...." He didn't allow me to say many words

"Good." I made an effort to continue.

"If Richard's behavior doesn't improve, he will be suspended for longer periods of time. I was hoping this meeting would help us, but I can see it hasn't." He stared at me as I continued. "We also have an alternative school for children we can not control at the local school." He looked at his wife, as if there was something wrong with me. Then he actually glared at me.

"I don't think you understand." He made his attempt to intimidate me with his mean look. I waited for the predictable, intimidating and always effective, clinched teeth from the bully. I'm sad to say, I didn't have to wait long. He stood up and put his hands on the top of my desk. I could only see his clinched teeth as he leaned toward me.

"I'll make this as plain as I can, man! If you call us again for anything, somebody's gonna get their ass beat." I was hoping he was referring to Richard, but I had a strong feeling it was my ass he was talking about. I was tired of his threats.

"Sir, this meeting's over. I don't have to sit here and listen to your threats. I was hoping you would help us. I made a mistake. You have a nice day." He was finished with me.

"That's not a threat, buddy. That's a fact." His ugly glare continued and my lack of response pushed him on. "And this meeting's over 'cause we're leavin', not 'cause you say so." I remained quiet as they left.

A few days later, word came to me that Richard was stealing bicycles from school. One of the students had seen where the bikes were hidden and came to me with the information. I called Richard to the office and after a few questions, he told me about stealing the bikes and he was planning to sell them. I called the police and Richard took them to where the stolen bicycles were hidden. They brought seven of the bikes back to school and they were returned to the owners. The police took Richard home.

The next morning, Richard's ugly stepfather was waiting for me when I arrived at school. He stood in the parking lot. He was a very frightening sight that early in the morning. He made it clear he wanted my attention.

"Hey, shit-head!" I continued walking toward the school building. When we are children, we are told to ignore the bully and name caller and they will stop or go away. I ignored him, but I really didn't think the old adage was going to work. I'm not sure if it had ever worked. He wasn't going away.

"Hey, I'm talkin' to you", he bellowed even louder. Even though I knew in my heart that ignoring him would probably make him even more aggressive. I gave it another try as I made my way closer to the safety of the school building and perhaps the protection of witnesses and numbers. I visualized my arms being ripped from my shoulders and I'm sure my steps quickened. I hoped my increase in walking speed was not too obvious. The speed of my heartbeat matched my foot speed as his voice filled the outside morning air.

"I know you made Richard confess to stealin' those bikes. He told me how you set him up. But you're mine now, so be lookin' for me."

I entered the school building with his words ringing in my ears. I watched him leave the parking lot from my office window and I had a small measure of relief for the moment. If he was gone, he couldn't hurt me. I didn't think, however, he was one of those talkers who never really do what they say they will do. He seemed determined and serious. I called security and reported the threat. It surprised me when I saw Richard in school that same day.

The next morning my new adventure continued. We had a visit from a court appointed, "guardian ad litem". These people are usually ladies appointed by the court system to follow up on child neglect and child abuse cases that have been placed under HRS and court control. That particular guardian was at school to see a child who had been sexually abused. While I was talking to the guardian in my office, Richard was brought into the school clinic because the teacher had seen a number of marks on him and she was concerned. I looked at the marks and could see Richard had been severely beaten the night before. He had cuts and bruises on his legs, back, buttocks, shoulders and neck. He had taken a serious beating. It was as bad as any I had seen.

The guardian went crazy with shock and anger when she saw Richard's injuries. I could tell she didn't have very much experience and she became extremely melodramatic. I realized later it was a mistake for me to involve her in Richard's situation, but at the time I thought that perhaps with her court appointed position, she would be able to help.

She surprised me when she asked for Richard's address and told me she wanted to visit the home. The guardian wanted to confront them over the abuse Richard had suffered. I advised her not to go alone and I called the police requesting they meet her at the school before she made her good intentioned visit. I tried to talk her into waiting for the police to accompany her, but she was too upset, angry and dramatic to listen. She said she didn't care how mean the stepfather was; it was her job to protect the children. I knew her over-zealous and blind concern would be trouble for her and it was.

The guardian arrived at Richard's address alone, and took her haughty and shallow authority up the stairs to the apartment. Richard's stepfather answered the door and after a brief one-sided introduction and exchange of words, he pushed her down the stairs, causing her to break her leg. The police came to the school and I sent them to the apartment. They arrived in time to assist the fallen crusader and called the rescue to come attend to her. Richard's father was gone. I received a letter two days later. The following is the actual wording of the letter.

"We know you are the one who called HRS and told them Richard's father beat him up. Which you know is bullshit. I was right about you. You are out to hurt our son and us. And I know why. It's because Richard is only half white, isn't it? Well, you S.O.B. now that I'm sure about you I'm going to make a phone call and make a complaint against you. I'm going to tell everything you've done and said to me, starting with the day I saw you. From now on every time you harass my son or us I'm going to make a complaint to the school board about you. And Richard is going to tell me if you are harassing him anymore just like he told me about Friday. You're nothing but a liar; you're lower than scum. I've told Richard he doesn't ever have to be scared of you telling us any more bullshit because he'll never ever get a spanking again for anything that happens at that sorry excuse of a school. So how do you like that you S.O.B.? I hope I run into you. I'd love to tell you just what I think of a scumbag like you. As of now I'm going to be rude and crude toward you. Watch and see if I don't. We are going to fight you all the way on everything from now on. No more cooperation from us ever. You can count on that. Nothing you can say can ever change what you've done to us. You started all this, now I'm going to see what I can do to make it harder for you to do this to anyone else. This is only the beginning."

The letter was not signed. Were people crazy, or what?

World's Finest Chocolates

Two days after the letter, I had another strange visit from Sally Dalton's stepsister, Betty. She told me her father had found out about a Mexican in the area who hated me and who had made threats against me. She thought Mr. Dalton had already made some type of deal with the man to hurt me or kill me. She wasn't sure, but she had a bad feeling about it. I had the same feeling. After she gave me the disturbing news she left me to ponder on my future, or lack of. I called my friend, Detective Ralph Moneyhun.

I was surprised when Ralph told me he already knew about the wild Mexican in the area. He knew his name and other stories about him. Ralph told me the police department considered him dangerous and we should take the information from Betty seriously. He encouraged me to carry a gun at school until they found the Mexican. Detective Moneyhun gave me a gun and a shoulder holster, so I carried a concealed weapon to school for two days. I really hated having that gun on me at school. It made me nervous, having it around the children. Even after Detective Moneyhun's warning, I couldn't keep the gun on me. I left it in my car. Detective Moneyhun called me and gave me these instructions:

"If he comes to school he's there to hurt you. Shoot him and call 911. Tell them you have just killed an intruder at school. Tell them to call me and don't talk to anyone until I get there. This guy is dangerous and serious." Those were unbelievable instructions for an elementary school principal.

I was nervous because of all the stress and problems around me, but the day had moved along at a normal pace. I was almost ready to go home when I had to answer the phone. I don't remember who was on the line or what they were saying, because when I said, hello I felt the presence as they entered my office. I turned with the phone to my ear and saw a sight that froze me to my bones.

The huge, malevolent Hispanic Neanderthal stood in my office only a few feet from me. He was even more ugly than he was before. I don't think I had ever been that afraid before in my life. He was wearing a small brief tank suit, like the professional wrestlers wore. He wore nothing else, no shirt, nor shoes. If he had been green, he would have passed for the "Hulk". He filled the doorway and blocked the normal exit from my office. His heavy breathing and flared nostrils revealed his intentions. He was there to hurt me. It was the ultimate moment of fear and intimidation. I was so sorry the gun was in the car, because I knew I needed it, and I knew I would have used it. I thought about the baseball bat under my desk, but I didn't think I could hurt him with it. I knew if he took it from me I would surely die. I didn't like it, but I was petrified and had never felt like that before. Once again, his voice added to my fear.

"Outside, chicken shit! The deal is that you fall so the whole neighborhood can see it." I yelled for Mrs. Highsmith to call the police. He didn't care. "Outside, now! You can either walk out there and take your whippin' or I can drag you out there and you'll still take the ass whippin'. Either way it's gonna happen."

I was so scared at that moment the only thing I could say was, "I'm not going outside with you." He directed his next statement to Mrs. Highsmith and one of our teachers, Mrs. Frye.

"Your boss is a real chicken shit fag, ladies. How ya'll like workin' with a queer?" He turned to me to add to my fear. "I'm just gonna break your legs this time." I thought of Mrs. Dalton when he mentioned breaking my legs. I had heard that before. It was her calling card. He had more. "There's a lot of folks want to see you hurt. You really piss people off, don't ya?" There were three ladies in the main office area at that time. I could see he was uncomfortable to have such an audience so late in the day. He looked frustrated with the time he had already spent and a sense of urgency came over him.

At that moment he stepped toward me and reached for me, trying to grab me over the desk. My fear gave me a hidden strength and I moved away and literally jumped over the desk. The move of desperation surprised both of us as he came over the desk after me.

About two hundred boxes of the World's Finest Chocolates from our failed candy sale project were stacked in the corner of my office. I stumbled over the boxes as I tried to get out of the room. I knew if he got his hands on me, I had no chance. Actually, you sometimes protect yourself better when you are scared and I was more than scared. My fear kept me free from his strong hands. His frustration grew.

"Just step outside and try to be a man for once in your life." He continued to taunt me, but I didn't respond, I just watched him. I was in a position to exit the back door of my office to another room. He realized he would have to chase me if he moved toward me again. He also knew he was running out of time and the police would be arriving soon. He lunged for me one more time.

I don't know why, but at first I didn't move. I guess I was frozen with fear. Instead, I picked up a box of the World's Finest Chocolates and threw it at him, then another and another. The boxes hitting him in the face and head actually stopped his advance for a second or two as he slapped at the projectiles. Candy bars were flying all over the office. He managed to grab my arm through the flurry of chocolate, but my sweaty arm and fear allowed me to break his hold. I ran through the back door of the office and into another room leading to an exit that would help me escape. He stepped into the main office where the ladies were still standing in shock, fear and disbelief. He turned and saw me at the end of the hallway, but he knew it would be impossible to get to me.

"Keep lookin' for me, queer boy. I'm comin' for ya.'

I watched him leave the office and go out the front door. I was relieved, but still shaken by the serious ordeal. I walked back to the main office where the three ladies were still waiting and concerned with my safety. Our campus security guard, Officer Stevens, came running into the building, as the Mexican drove away. After I called security to report the incident, I joined the three ladies in the main office. Mrs. Frye approached me with a true look of concern on her face.

"Mr. Reynolds, you were white as a ghost. I don't think I've ever seen anyone that scared before."

"Thank you so much, Mrs. Frye, for your colorful observation." Her assessment will stay with me forever.

I was disappointed when the school security told me I would have to press charges against my attacker on my own. He had not actually hurt me and it would be up to me to make the complaint. My effort turned out to be a joke, as far as I was concerned. When I tried to tell what took place and the trouble I was having, I was asked by the State Attorney's office to meet with the Mexican in the presence of a mediator and see if we could work out our differences. I couldn't believe it. I told the State Attorney that the Mexican hadn't stolen my dog; he wanted to break my legs. I was told I had not been injured and there was not much that could be done. I was disappointed in both systems, the legal one and the school. I called Detective Moneyhun for advice. He had tried to locate the Mexican, but the beast and his family were gone.

The Lude Mutiny

The twenty days had passed and it was time for Steven and Tommy Lude to return from their stay at the alternative school. All three of the Lude children stood at the front counter in the main office. Behind them stood, Mrs. Lude and my nemeses, Alvin Lester. Ms. Lude requested a meeting with me and I agreed. We all walked to my office, including, to my surprise, Alvin Lester. I stopped him at the door.

"I'm meeting with Mrs. Lude. This does not concern you so please wait outside. In fact, I don't think you need to be on the campus at all." He then set the tone for the day with an unbelievable statement.

"Her name ain't Lude no more. It's Mrs. Lester. She's my old lady, now."

Once more I found I couldn't believe what I had just heard. He was eighteen, at the most, and she was thirty, at the least. He was right about one thing; she was his old lady. He continued to dumbfound me.

"I want all their records changed today and their last name changed to Lester."

Were people crazy, or what? After all the time in my professional life I had spent with the crazies, I was still amazed at the stupidity that continued to surround me. What an idiot I had standing in front of me.

"Do you have the adoption papers and the change of name documents with you?

The idiot continued. "Don't hand me that crap. She said it was all right. She's their mother. We want 'em changed. I told her you'd give me a hard time." I knew it would be senseless to talk to the pretend "daddy", so I turned my attention to the other idiot and new Mrs. Lester.

"You must know I cannot change their names without the proper papers. We will call them what ever you want, but I can not change the official records until we get the correct and legal papers authorizing us to do so." Crystal, the youngest, surprised me and joined the conversation.

"I don't want my name changed, Mr. Reynolds." Then Tommy added his feelings.

"Me either." There was a small sign of a Lude children rebellion in the air.

"You'll have to talk to your mother. That's a family matter. Your names will not be changed at school." With me there, Tommy had more confidence and he added more of his thoughts.

"Call our real daddy, Mr. Reynolds. He won't let 'em change our names."

Alvin Lester had a full-fledged mutiny on his dirty hands and he didn't like it at all. He was mad and it was easy to see he was more than immature and crazy. He stood up and stomped out of my office. The new Mrs. Lester followed him and the children went to class.

After that day the behavior of the Lude children was worse than ever. Even Crystal began to cause more trouble than she had before. Their mother gave us no cooperation at all. She would not return my calls and would not respond to the letters I sent home to her. My last effort was this letter:

Mrs. Lude,

Your children will not be allowed to return to school until we meet to discuss the problems we are having. This is very serious and it cannot continue. If you do not respond to this request, I will report you to HRS for neglect.

The next morning the entire family sat in my office again. It didn't take but a second for me to figure out why Mrs. Lude had not been around for a while. Her left eye was black and swollen shut. She looked as if she had been taking beatings on a regular basis. I tried to direct the conversation to Mrs. Lude, but Lester made it clear he was the spokesman for the family and he was running the show. He was very angry with me.

"First, I want to know why you keep callin' her Mrs. Lude? Her name is Mrs. Lester. I already told you that. You even write it on letters you send to her. I think you're doin' that shit on purpose."

I enjoyed the fact he was upset with my insensitivity to his wishes. I knew from that moment on, I would never call her Mrs. Lester. She would always be "Mama Lude" to me. His profanity helped me end his moment as the family leader.

"I am not discussing any of this with you. Your verbal abuse and improper language will not be tolerated in this office. I will talk to their mother about the situation and she can tell you the details, if she chooses. Now, leave the school, or I will have you arrested for disrupting the school process." As usual, my heart was pounding and I thought I might have to defend myself against an eighteen year old pretending to be an adult. I knew I had the authority to have him arrested, but I also knew he was crazy enough not to care. He continued to try and run the show.

"You're a nigger lovin' asshole. Let's get our kids out of this crazy school." He gave directions to his new family, but Mrs. Lude resisted and her first comment of the day took her immature husband's attention away from me.

"They have to be in school." It was a weak statement, but she had taken a stand. Alvin Lester was mad at everyone now. He glared at her.

"He can't do nothin' to ya, stupid." He was too ignorant to understand she didn't want the children to stay home. The school was her relief and she was also afraid of the thought of neglect charges I had mentioned to her. He crumbled.

"This is bullshit. You do what you want. They're your stupid kids anyway."

I thought to myself, "What a pitiful example this new stepfather was for the three Lude children who were already mentally disturbed." He left the office and I thought about thanking Mrs. Lude for saving me, but it was only a thought. The "asshole" chant she had directed in the parking lot would always limit my compassion. She promised the children would behave. I wanted her out of the office so I thanked her and sent the children to class. I knew they would not change, but I knew they needed to be in school. They were pitiful and tormented by their mother and her child groom. The school gave them the few positive moments they had in the awful days of their lives. I had to continue to make myself remember I was in the "caring" business.

For the next three days, I received complaints from teachers that Alvin Lester was showing up at their classrooms and wanting to talk to his stepchildren. He argued with Tommy in front of the teacher and students, sat down in a desk near Crystal and threatened Steven's teacher, Ms. Keller, with bodily harm. Each time I was made aware of his intrusion, he would get away before I could confront him. The teachers were alerted to the possibility of him coming on the school grounds. I met with the county security so the problem would be recorded and I wrote Alvin Lester a letter informing him he was not permitted to be anywhere on the school campus and that he would be considered a trespasser if he made another visit. I gave the letter to Mr. Adam from the county security and he delivered it to Mr. Lester. Mr. Adam also gave him a verbal warning to stay away from the school.

The same day the letter was delivered, I was standing in front of the school, helping direct traffic during dismissal, when I felt the presence of someone behind me on the sidewalk. I turned to see Alvin Lester only a few feet away from me. I didn't know how long he had been there, but the thought of him trying to sneak up on me made me rather uneasy. When you're the principal of an elementary school you should not have to worry about people sneaking up on you. He was right on me and again my heart raced in my chest. I didn't want to show any fear, but I knew he could tell his presence disturbed me. I'm sure he interpreted that as fear. Cowards like him live to scare others.

In front of all the students and parents, he made another stand as he tore into little pieces, what appeared to be the letter I had sent him. He threw the pieces of paper at me.

"That's what I think about you and your letter."

Then he spit at me, hitting my shirt. It was too much for me to handle and I didn't control myself very well. Getting spit upon is the supreme insult. Once again, the old professionalism flew the coop. As they say, "I lost it". I grabbed Alvin Lester and moved him backwards until the outside brick wall of the school stopped our movement. His back and head slammed against the bricks. When we hit the hard wall I felt and heard all the air leave his body. If you have ever had the breath knocked out of you, you understand what happened. The feeling is awful and frightening. It was easy to see my actions had surprised and hurt Lester. He moved away from me in a sliding motion, keeping contact with the brick wall as he struggled to catch his breath. His fight was no longer with me at that moment. He needed to reclaim the air he had lost. For the first time he looked like the young eighteen-year-old boy he was, and for a brief moment I even felt sorry for him as I watched his pain, but only for a second.

Parents came to assist me, or to be part of the excitement, but the short physical confrontation was over. I continued to watch Lester struggle and move farther away from me. Two fathers, standing near me on the sidewalk asked me if I wanted them to stop him from leaving, but I just wanted him to leave. We watched him walk out into the street and out of sight. I called security and reported the incident. Sleep was illusive that night. There is something awful and demeaning about being spat upon, but as an educator, I should have had better control.

I did not see Alvin Lester for a long time after that day. Mrs. Lude did meet with me a number of times. Sometimes at her request and other times at mine. She never mentioned my physical confrontation with Lester. I don't think she ever knew about it. Each time I saw her she looked like she had been beaten. Her face was always cut, bruised or scratched. Even though she had been so awful to me, I didn't want to see any human being take such abuse and punishment. The beatings were aging her and she also had the look of a "user". I was getting quite good at recognizing the drug abusers. She sat in my office and for some stupid reason I wanted her to know I would still help her if she needed it.

"Mrs. Lude, your eye and cheek really look bad. What happened?" She did not hesitate.

"Alvin hit me."

"Well, it looks bad. Is there something I can do to help you? You don't have to take that kind of abuse from him." My concern was short lived with her reply.

"You oughta see him. I got in a few good licks, myself." So much for the role of the "concerned principal".

Roofers

The last bus moved away from the school and the school day was coming to an end for us all. Mrs. Highsmith told me I had a phone call. I went against my better instincts and took the call.

"This is Bill Reynolds." The voice on the other end of the phone was yelling. He must have thought I couldn't hear him, but I could hear him perfectly.

"Is this the principal?"

"Yes it is. Who is this?"

"This is Tommy Lee. My daughter, Linda, goes to your school." He was still yelling. "I'm at the police station downtown. I've been arrested and I didn't know who else to call. We got no phone at the house so I can't call my wife. I need someone to take Linda home and tell her mother where I am. I met you last week and I thought you might help me out here." There was no way I wanted to get involved at all. He had more to say.

"Linda's somewhere at the school. She's probably waiting for me to pick her up out front. Please find her and take her home. Tell my wife what has happened. She'll know what to do. Gotta go." The phone went dead and so did my opportunity to go home. Linda was waiting at the front of the school.

I stopped my Navy blue bug in front of the house Linda pointed out to me. I noticed a group of roofers on a house across the street. Linda jumped out of my car and ran up to the house and tried to open the front door. It was locked. She knocked, but there was no answer. Linda moved away from the front door and went around the side of the house disappearing toward the back of the house. I stepped to the side where she ran, but could not see her. I knew I should have gone back and waited at the car and why I didn't was beyond me. I stepped toward the back of the house hoping to find the child I was responsible for because of the phone call from her father. I turned the corner of the house and found myself face-to-face with a pretty young woman. She looked to be in her late twenties. She wore tight white short-shorts and a sheer blouse that was tied at the waist, exposing her stomach. Linda was standing behind the young woman. The sudden meeting startled me, but for some strange reason it really scared the woman. She screamed. I don't mean a little scream. I mean a horror movie, bloodcurdling scream. Then Linda screamed, too. I wanted to join them, because they both really scared me, too.

"I didn't mean to scare you ma'am. I was looking for Linda." Before she could respond or I could introduce myself and give her the information she needed to hear, a voice from behind me interrupted our strange meeting and conversation.

"What ya doin' back here, mister, scarin' the little girl?" I turned to see the entire group of roofers standing behind me. The man doing the talking was nothing but muscles and he was there to show off for the pretty young woman. I was getting rather good at being able to speak quickly when I was afraid. I hit them with my usual introduction.

"I'm the principal of the school. I was just bringing Linda home for her father." The young knot of a man didn't care.

"That still don't give you the right to just walk around the house to see what you can see, does it?" He looked at the pretty young woman with "want' in his bloodshot eyes.

"You okay, Brenda?"

Brenda and Linda, let's rhyme those names. I took his moment of attending to Brenda as my moment to take over and try to calm the aggressive direction the conversation had taken. I was also getting good at finding my openings. I addressed Brenda, too.

"Your husband called me and asked me to bring Linda home. He couldn't call you, so I guess the school was the next best thing. I'm sorry if I scared you. I'd like to speak to you privately, if you don't mind." The young roofer chimed in.

"I'll bet you would. You come around here with your tie on actin' like you can do what ever you want. Go on back to school and bother somebody else." Was he crazy or what?

When people are like he was you have to be careful, because there was no telling when they would explode. I decided I didn't need that private moment with the screamer. She was probably as crazy as the roofer and no telling when she would explode either.

"Your husband's in jail. He needs you to take care of it. Have a nice day."

I stepped away from the three of them and began to move through the other roofers who had followed the talker. The way they had lined up made it look like I was moving through a short six-man gauntlet. As I walked past them I tried not to make any eye contact with any of them. I didn't want to be forced to answer that troublesome question of, "What you lookin' at?" Those four words have caused a great amount pain, sorrow and suffering for many men throughout time. I knew I was in a perfect setting for such an altercation if I made eye contact with any of them. I knew it wouldn't take much from me to cause the explosion.

They didn't really move out of my way as I walked, but there was enough room so I didn't have to make any physical contact. Bumping into someone has been known to cause as much misery as the four dreaded words. Then, a voice broke the tense moment. It came from the group of men as I was passing.

"Ain't you coach Reynolds?" It was like a voice from heaven. When I heard that question I felt I could turn and face the roofers. I focused in on a young man. I knew his face, but it had matured from the child I once knew. His name even popped into my spinning head.

"Troy, it has been a long time since your elementary school days." His face lit up like a candle. I could see he loved the fact I remembered him. He stepped forward, leaving the others and shook my hand. It was a manly and most welcomed handshake. He walked with me to my Beetle Bug. He remembered my little car.

"I remember when you got this bug. It used to be green, didn't it?" I smiled. It was a genuine smile for him, but also a smile of relief for me. A former student from my days as an elementary physical education teacher had saved me from possible pain at the hands of the talker.

"That's right, it was green. I had it painted last year."

"How old is this car?"

"Fifteen years old." He smiled and shook his head.

I shook his hand again and got into the car. I turned the key and nothing happened. My bug was dead. Troy and his fellow roofers had to give my car a push to get me on my way. The talker didn't help. I told Mrs. Highsmith the next day to find out where the caller was calling from before she gave me the phone. We both got a chuckle out of that. Were people crazy, or what?

Human Party Hat

Mrs. McWilliams stood at my office door early that morning. "Good morning Mr. Reynolds. I need to talk to you about a kindergarten student who has been with us for only two weeks. His name is James Walker and he's in Mrs. Brown's kindergarten class." Mrs. McWilliams always made sure I was aware of the teacher's needs. "You haven't seen him yet because Mrs. Brown has been trying to take care of the problem without bothering you. You really need to observe this child."

If Mrs. McWilliams thought I needed to get involved, I knew I did. I trusted her judgment at all times. It was comforting to trust my fellow workers. It made going to work each day much easier. We both walked to Mrs. Brown's classroom to take a look at our new student, James.

Mrs. Brown was at the piano conducting a morning sing along. I am always amazed at the many talents our teachers possess. A blonde haired boy sat in a chair next to the piano while the other children sat around on the carpeted floor. Mrs. McWilliams nodded in the direction of the child.

"That's James in the chair."

He noticed us looking at him and he rolled out of the chair onto the floor. The music stopped as Mrs. Brown reached for him.

"Excuse us Mr. Reynolds, we have a problem staying in our seat today." James rolled away from her, stood up and ran over to the aquarium tank on the other side of the room. As I watched, he began licking the side of the tank as the fish swam next to the glass. I looked at Mrs. Brown.

"We're here to see your new little friend in action and see if we can help. Don't stop playing on our account. Just let him do what he does."

Mrs. Brown continued with the sing along as James put on a show for the visitors. As I watched his strange behavior, there were moments when he would stop and his entire body would quiver. It only lasted a few seconds and I was sure it was something he could not control. It was not part of his show. He knew we were watching him and he knew what he was doing. It was a game and he knew how to play. He was enjoying the attention. I'm sure the sing along ended sooner than usual, but Mrs. Brown was nervous about the disruptive James. Mrs. Brown had some interesting information for me.

"The real strange thing, Mr. Reynolds, is that James is probably the smartest one in the class. He reads, knows his letters, and is the best with numbers. He just can't color inside the lines. His fine motor skills are very weak, but he is advanced in all the other areas. His papers are a mess, but he has all the right answers." Mrs. Brown stepped closer to me so she could whisper to me. "He's a strange little character, but he's very smart."

I assured Mrs. Brown she didn't have to struggle with James and to let me know if he became a major problem. We never want the entire class to suffer because of one disruptive child. Educators believe in the philosophy of the Star Trek Vulcan, Mr. Spock: "The needs of the many outweigh the needs of the few." I told Mrs. Brown I would contact James' parents and see if they were aware of his behavior and if they could help us.

Mrs. McWilliams talked to James' mother later that day who said both she and her husband would meet with me when they picked James up at the kindergarten dismissal time. They arrived on time and once again I found myself amazed at how crazy people can be.

James ran into my office first. He scared me for a moment, because I was writing and was not expecting a noisy intruder. I wasn't sure how many surprises my pounding heart could take. James' father walked into my office next. I couldn't believe my eyes. He wore only a pair of silk running shorts with waist high slits on each side. He wore no shirt, no shoes. James' mother walked in last.

She was much taller than her husband. She wore shorts, no shoes and a tank shirt that was three sizes too big for her. It was obvious she was not wearing a bra and her bare breasts were exposed on both sides of the oversized tank top. To add to the obscene fashion show, she looked to be at least nine months pregnant and ready to drop the child at any moment. Her only interest at that moment was getting off her feet. She literally fell into one of the chairs in front of my desk. She made her thoughts clear as soon as she was comfortable in the chair and her body parts stopped quivering.

"I'm really miserable, mister, so let's make this quick. I ain't too happy about getting' out of the car as it is." I was just as miserable as she was. Even though I was shocked at their appearance, I wanted to greet them as if it was a normal parent conference. I had no idea what I was getting into.

"I do appreciate you both coming in to see me on such a short notice." James' father was still standing. When he reached out to shake my hand he intentionally made his chest muscles flex up and down. He then added to my amazement with his first statement.

"We know James is a real pain in the ass, but he's crazy like that at home too." His wife was offended.

"He ain't crazy, you're crazy." I knew right at that moment, they were all crazy. Dad looked at me and went on.

"He's crazy, just like her.' He rolled his eyes toward his wife, as if I wouldn't realize whom he was talking about. "I'm thinkin' about havin' her put away after the baby comes." I was getting too much information after one handshake and a dancing chest. It was her turn.

"He's the crazy one. If anybody's gonna get put away, it's him." He retaliated.

"She's on dope and I'm sure this new baby will be as crazy as James. She was on dope with him too." I had heard enough.

"Please sit down. You will have to take care of your personal problems elsewhere. This is not the time or place. We're here to talk about James' improper behavior here at school." Hearing me mention his name, James rolled on the floor, but neither one of them acknowledged his action nor his presence. Mr. Walker remained standing. I told them we would like permission to test James to see if we could help with his problems in the classroom. Mrs. Walker didn't like my suggestion. The look on her face was what I would call, down right evil.

"He ain't retarded!" She was mad and glaring at me. I never have been very good at staring people down, unless they were a first grader. I didn't want to look at her husband either, but he was the better choice. She was awful to look at. I took a deep breath and tried to stay as professional as I could.

"We know he's not retarded. No one thinks that at all. In fact, he's probably the smartest one in the class. His behavior seems to be the problem." She continued the glare.

"No testing. They tested my brother and he's still messed up because of it. James acts fine at home. Someone here at this school must be makin' him act like that." Her husband couldn't stand it. He was still standing and looked ready to explode.

"See how crazy she is?" He looked at her with his eyes wide open to get her attention. "Do you think this man really believes that James is only nuts here at school? You are crazy." She looked away and ignored him in silence. James was still rolling on the floor. He wasn't hurting anything so, like his parents, I didn't respond to his actions. I'm sorry to say I was more interested in the crazy couple in front of me.

Then I made a huge mistake as the bizarre encounter continued. I asked Mr. Walker to sit down one more time and I was very sad I made the request. The moment his little silk running shorts hit the seat of the chair, his genitals popped out from under the shorts and lay, exposed on the top of his leg. He acted like he didn't know what had happened, but he had to know. His wife was still mad and looking away from him and did not see the exposure at first. It was up to me.

"Sir, could you fix yourself?" I nodded toward his revealed privates. He looked down.

"Oh! Sorry man. I can't seem to keep those boys in there." He tucked "them" back under his shorts. His wife turned her head as he was fixing the problem. She shook her head with disgust.

"He loves it when that happens. He does it on purpose and he says I'm the crazy one." She continued shaking her head. I wanted to shake my head too and I wanted them gone. I was actually afraid to stay in the same room with those two insane people. James was the most normal of the three, but it was more than easy to see he didn't have a chance to be anything but crazy. He was still rolling on the floor. I made an attempt to end the pointless meeting.

"Please consider having James tested and we will all work together on improving his behavior. At this time, we may have to modify his schedule at school until his behavior improves." James stopped rolling on the floor and stood up next to his mother. He grabbed her cheeks and kissed her on the lips. He then put his head against her stomach as if he was listening to the baby she carried. He kissed her stomach. That small level of affection and sanity, if you can believe it, took the four of us to a new level of insanity.

James climbed up onto the chair and then on up his mother's body until he was on her shoulders. My amazement grew as I watched him work his way onto the top of her head. He put both his feet on her shoulders and sat with his butt on the top of her head. I stared at him as he sat there like a "party hat". She began moving her head from side-to-side to keep him balanced as if they were perfecting a circus act. I looked at her husband. He watched her too. She interrupted the deep trance of amazement I had fallen into.

"He'll be better tomorrow and no testing." Her human hat was balanced and stable as she talked. "I don't think the school has tried very hard to work with James. He's only been here for a week or so." Her hat remained. I couldn't take anymore.

"Mrs. Walker, does all this really seem normal to you? Your son is sitting on your head and we are trying to have a conversation." She was angry and scared me with another evil look.

"What's normal in my house may not be normal in yours." It just wasn't that simple to me.

"Mrs. Walker, this is not normal in the civilized world." With that comment, she took off her "party hat", struggled to get out of the chair and directed her husband.

"Let's get out of here. He ain't gonna help us. He hates James and I know he's been lookin' at my tits." I had no reply for her statement as she walked out of the room. As Mr. Walker walked out behind her he looked back at me.

"She's just wacked out, man. I know it's hard not to look at them big titties. Catch ya later." Were people crazy, or what?

Rambo Dad

Parenthood was in rare form that week. We had another pregnant fifth grader, three of our teachers announced their own pregnancies and someone found another dead newborn baby in the dumpster at the apartments near the school.

The mentally disturbed father of one of our students revisited Vietnam in his dreams and tied his son, Chris, to a tree in the woods a block from the school. He was going to use the child for target practice with a hunting bow and arrows. Two boys alerted us and we called the police. I went with the boys and we reached Chris before the police arrived. I was very nervous, because I didn't see his father as I untied the young man from the tree. I don't think you hear arrows coming before they hit you. As I walked with Chris back to the school he said his father had tied him to the tree because he needed to work on his aim. Then he left. He didn't shoot at Chris, but the boy was afraid his father was coming back He was shaken by the early morning ordeal and I felt sorry and sad for him. How do you go to school and do your best with such worries on your mind?

The police picked Chris' father up later in the same woods. He was dressed in full fatigues and boots and he was carrying a hunting bow with arrows. To add to the insanity, he had painted his face Rambo style. I'd say all of that was pretty scary for a third grader.

The police informed me the man had been arrested before for domestic violence against his wife. It seemed he would have dreams about being at war, wake up in the middle of the night thinking he was still in the jungles of Vietnam, and beat her because he thought she was the enemy.

Now, I don't know about such things. I was not in Vietnam. I have heard that many veterans of that war still suffer from conditions caused by stress and the mental return to the jungles has happened to many. I just hoped people like Chris' father wouldn't use their past as a convenient means to act crazy and hurt the people around them. I probably would have thought about the situation with Chris all that day, but that was the same day I met Anwar and his mother. That new adventure wiped Chris right out of my head until another time.

The Anwar Complex

Anwar and his mother had moved from Miami to escape an abusive relationship with Anwar's stepfather and her fourth husband. Anwar's real father was dead. Anwar was a fifth grader and much bigger than his mother. They both had the same facial features: blue eyes, full lips, moon-pie shaped face, and black hair. As she talked about her tale of woe, he couldn't keep his hands off of her. He rubbed her back. She made him stop. He kissed her cheek, forehead and lips. She made him stop. He reached and squeezed her breasts. She slapped his hand. He did it again. She slapped him again. It was too crazy for me.

"Stop doing that to your mother. Young boys don't do such things to their mother." He was mad and he sat down, but he didn't stop. "Don't let him do that to you. He's really too big to be acting like this." I could tell she didn't like me saying what I said, but it was her first meeting with me and she seemed cautious and did not respond. Anwar was calm, but still mad. She registered him into our school that day.

It was only a matter of a day or two before Anwar became a serious problem. His language was vulgar and outrageous for a fifth grader or anybody for that matter. He would not leave the girls alone in the classroom, halls, cafeteria, or on the playground.

He would try to join the girl's activities and somehow he seemed to manage to touch them improperly. Anwar was a fifth grade "masher" and "copped a feel" at every opportunity. He was absolutely terrible and the teachers, students and parents all complained about his actions.

Getting his mother involved was a joke. She defended him at every turn, and in every situation blamed the school, his real father, his stepfather and anyone else she could think of at the moment. Anwar knew she would defend him and that gave him the green light for all his awful actions. And to add fuel to the fire, he was extremely gifted and had the highest IQ of any of our students in our fifth grade classes. He was much smarter than his mother and that added to his ability to control many of the situations we were involved in.

During one of our pointless meetings she told me Anwar's real father was gifted, too. She also gave me some information I didn't care to hear, information I would later use against her. I asked Anwar to sit out in the main office so his mother and I could talk without his ritual of touching her. Anwar was not a little boy. He was an oversized fifth grader and I had to question her about his strange and aggressive behavior. To this day I have no idea why she told me what she did.

"Why do you think he has to touch you like he does and have all of your attention no matter what you are doing? He really needs to stop and you need to be sure he does."

I must have caught her in a moment of guilt and true confession, because she was ready to talk. If I had known the information I was getting ready to hear, I would have asked Mrs. McWilliams to sit with us.

"I guess I have spoiled him. It's really my fault." That was the first time she had said anything was her fault. She went on and a new adventure began.

"He sleeps with me, you know?" Her statement surprised me and I wanted to say, "No, I didn't know." I did know one thing and that was I wanted her to continue talking and she did.

"We started sleeping together for safety reasons and comfort a few years ago and now it has become a habit for us both." She hesitated, as if she was sorry she had told me. Then, when she opened her mouth again I realized her hesitation was only to think about her next bizarre statement.

"He's always been crazy about my boobs. I guess it's a nursing thing." She was dead serious as I looked at her. I didn't know what to say. I just stared at her trying to stay focused on her eyes and not look elsewhere. She was not through with her shocking revelations.

"I guess my need to sleep in the nude has added to the problem." I wanted to scream: "You guess it adds to the problem?" I let her continue. In fact, I couldn't wait for her to continue.

"I think he touches me during the night. He thinks I'm his, I guess. He loves to lay his head on my bare boobs." I was at my limit. It was over for me. I looked for Alan Funt and his Candid Camera. That afternoon I called HRS and gave them the story as it was presented to me. Anwar and his mother moved away that week.

Yellow Pinto

The neglect and abuse was driving me crazy. Protecting the students and teachers became an everyday endeavor. Over fifteen percent of the student body had been sexually abused by adults. It was difficult to ask a child to take a spelling test if the child was worried about the abuse that awaited him or her at home.

Our new cafeteria manager was fishing off the Trout River Bridge over the weekend and she was hit by a truck and knocked into the water. She was dead. The shock of such a tragedy set the tone for another interesting week. I really wasn't ready to greet a new parent that morning, but as I said before, that's what we did. I should have locked the door to my office. My smile and greeting would be only temporary after I met the "Crumrines".

A short and extremely overweight woman dressed entirely in black walked into my office followed by four children. An odor also entered the room with them. I wasn't sure which one was giving off the smell or if it was a combination of the five of them. Either way, it was bad.

"Good morning, Mr. Reynolds, I'm Mary Crumrine. This is Samuel, Joshua, Charity and this is Hope. She's the oldest. Hope won't be comin' to your school."

Hope was dressed in black, with black lips and black fingernails. She was short and overweight like her mother. Hope joined the conversation.

"I'm in the tenth grade, but I'm already eighteen." Hope seemed very proud of her longevity in the school system. Mother interrupted Hope's moment in the sun.

"She tells everybody that. She's just a little slow, that's all, and we have moved around a lot. She's had some real bad teachers." Hope smiled in agreement with her mother's statement about her teachers. I thought to myself, "Let's be sure to blame a poor teacher somewhere." Mother went on.

"Now, this here is Joshua. He's the smart one." Joshua seemed harmless enough as he smiled at me and bathed in his mother's praise. At least his lips were not black. At a later date he would, however, terrorize the school. The introductions continued.

"And this is Charity. She's the baby. She's had some real problems in school. She ate paint chips in an old house we lived in when she was a little baby and got lead poisoning. She ain't been right since." Charity was quiet and she did have a different look to her. Mother had one more to introduce to me.

"Then there's Samuel. He's the bad one." What high expectations she had for Samuel. Some people really are crazy. "He's in the fifth grade and he has an awful bad temper. You just call me if he hits anybody. I'll take care of the beatin's. We don't want you beatin' our kids."

I didn't want to continue my first meeting with the Crumrines, so I said, "Welcome and I hope they enjoy the school." I didn't know what else to say. I had quite a number of times I didn't know what to say. My first encounter with them was just that, the first of many.

The Ludes Tell All

It wasn't long before the stories began to roll off the lips of the Lude children. We heard of the awful fights at night and the police arresting their new stepfather, Alvin Lester. For a few months we heard stories each day about physical encounters taking place in the Lester-Lude apartment. The stories didn't come from the Lude children only.
Parents and other students all knew of the Lester-Lude family feuds. At least the two adults were staying away from school and the children were attending on a regular basis. I felt we were the safest place for the children.

At Mrs. McWilliams' urging, we tried to work with the troubled Lude children without involving their crazy mother at all. It was difficult, but Mrs. McWilliams and the teachers tried to give some pleasant moments to the three Ludes. They didn't make it easy to find those moments, but we did the best we could. We knew they were going home to a sad and awful situation so we made a strong effort to make their time with us a positive experience. It was hard to try and save children who were with us only seven hours a day and then went home to seventeen hours of hell.

Then one morning, Mrs. Lude stood at the front desk signing her three children out early. I couldn't believe my eyes. She was very pregnant and she looked as if she would have the baby at any second. I was shocked because with all the wild stories we had heard from the Lude children and the general public, no one had ever mentioned the fact that she was with child. She could hardly walk and her discomfort was most obvious. Her once thin face, was full from her weight gain and I probably would not have recognized her if Tommy had not been standing with her. I also recognized her black eye that seemed to be a permanent feature. She looked at me with hate in her eyes and walked away from the front desk and out of the building followed by her three children.

Mrs. Highsmith informed me Mrs. Lude had withdrawn her children and they were transferring to another school. At the moment it seemed like good news. About three days later, Tommy came to me with a wild story about the trials and tribulations of the Lester-Ludes.

They had not gone to another school. The stepfather had lost his job and the entire family had been evicted from their apartment and they were supposedly living in the woods in a yellow Ford Pinto. The three Lude children were sleeping on the ground next to the car and the Lester family, new baby and all, were sleeping in the car. Lester was stealing during the day so the baby could have a blanket and other baby things. I knew Tommy was telling me his sad story because he didn't want to return to his new life-style and like his mother, he knew I would help. He was right. Mrs. McWilliams made sure of that. As much as I disliked Mr. Lester, the newborn baby needed a chance to sleep in a bed, as well as the other three children did. After another reminder from Mrs. McWilliams of my obligation to the children and my fellow man, I called HRS again.

Tommy had given me information about where they would be during the day and the HRS alerted the police. The other members of the Lude-Lester family were located and the HRS was able to assist them with some immediate needs for the children and the baby.

Three days later we heard the children were going to attend another school and I thought perhaps the HRS had helped them relocate and find housing or perhaps they had taken the four children away from the abusive and neglectful environment. We received a report from other students that the children had registered at another school, but they were still living in the Pinto. I made contact with the other school and it was true, they had registered, but they had not attended. The Lude-Lester homeless family was gone.

Coca-Cola Test

All three of the Crumrine children who attended our school were insane, but what else could they be? Samuel terrorized the fifth grade teachers and students in every way possible. He was a thief and a bully. He was intimidating, disrespectful and anything else you could imagine. Joshua, the gifted one, used his high intellect to tease and torment others. He found weaknesses in other students and took advantage of them whenever he could. He was absolutely heartless and he reveled in the discomfort of others

Charity was actually not a behavior problem. She did nothing but sleep all day and eat like a horse at lunchtime. She needed medical help. Even the oldest, Hope, who didn't go to our school, drove us crazy in the afternoons when she came to walk the others home. She would cause major disturbances with the other students, teachers and parents.

Hope would fight with the smaller elementary students, curse at teachers and argue with parents who were waiting for their children to be dismissed. I had to call the police two times and have her removed from the school grounds. We finally had to write her a letter stating if she came back to the school campus she would be treated as a trespasser and she would be arrested.

I met with Mrs. Crumrine hoping she would be able to help us with her children.   Nothing we did was working.   She refused our suggestions that we help get medical treatment for Charity.   She refused to have Joshua tested for emotional problems. She said she was doing all she could to make Samuel behave, but she was very angry about how unfairly I had treated her daughter Hope. After she refused any of my suggestions, she told me how much she disliked me. At that moment the awful and insane Crumrine misadventure began.   I'm not sure why I even listened to her, but I did. I guess I was just too tired to walk out of my own office.

"Mr. Reynolds, I'm trying to keep my husband from finding out about all the problems here at this school with the children. I'm supposed to be the one who takes care of these things and I'm not doing a very good job. The sin of my failure will be on me and the punishment will be severe." Once again I didn't know what to say so I gave her time to continue if she had more. She did. "He's been measuring the Coke bottle again so I know he's been talking to God." I had no idea what she meant or where we were headed, but again I waited for more. "You see, he leaves an open bottle of Coke in the icebox. He marks the level of coke. If the coke is below the line, he knows someone has been drinking it. It is a test for us all."

I knew once again, I was sitting at my desk looking at another crazy person with children in her care. In fact, she was a crazy woman living with a crazy man raising crazy kids. What else could the children be? Once again, the well-known educational saying about following a crazy child home and a crazy mama answers the door, held true.   Mrs. Crumrine continued with more information I didn't want to hear.

"The last time the coke went down it was our oldest son who got the bullwhip and he ran away. That was two years ago. He was seventeen then. He hitchhiked back to Virginia and lives with his real mother now. He wasn't mine, but I loved him just as much as I love the others. I was sorry when he was punished like that." I still had nothing to say, but she didn't seem to care. She was in her own world and wrapped in her strange tale of woe. She wanted me to listen.

"The Bible tells us women to serve the man, that's his favorite passage. We read it everyday. Are you a Christian man, Mr. Reynolds?" Her question ended my silence.

"I would like to think so, Mrs. Crumrine, but women as servants and using a bullwhip are not part of my spiritual thoughts." She really didn't care about my answer. I'm not even sure why she took the time to ask me anyway. I could tell she was not listening to me.

"A husband could kill his wife for many different reasons. I will not give him a reason to do so." I was drained and could not take anymore. I knew my limits when it came to dealing with the crazies.

"Mrs. Crumrine, I don't need to know anything else about your private life. Please, you have told me too much. We need help with your children. If we find we are unable to control them at school, starting tomorrow, I will use my authority and send them to the alternative school." She was mad again and she walked out of my office. For some reason I wanted to see that coke bottle marking, bullwhip man. I would soon get my wish.

The Cane Toss

Each day at school was unique and interesting. The excitement and anticipation would envelop you and even though it was scary and hectic at times, it kept you alert and ready for what was to come. Some days were more insane than others, but all were wild to a degree. I didn't want to become comfortable with the unusual and bizarre, but it became understood and expected.

Mrs. McWilliams and I were talking to Carol, a twelve-year-old fifth grader, about keeping her hands off the boy's behinds at school. Carol was more of a woman than a child. She was short, but physically developed. Her tight shorts and shirts revealed her mature body. She was driving the boys crazy with her pinches and squeezes. Mrs. McWilliams usually took care of such situations, but for some reason we were both with Carol in my office.

"Carol, why do you keep touching the boys?" Carol looked at Mrs. McWilliams.

"I just can't help it. I just love them butts. Mama says, it's fine to like butts, but don't suck their things. They will try to talk you into sucking their things, but don't. It's fine to like butts." We let Carol go back to class. Mrs. McWilliams could talk to her later.

As Carol walked out of my office, Mrs. McWilliams and I looked at each other in amazement. I had no idea at the time I would soon be eye-to-eye with the one who talked to God and carried a bullwhip. Mr. Crumrine was already at the door of Joshua's classroom, without a visitor's pass. This was a serious problem if you were to have a safe school climate that protects the students and the teachers from outside disturbances and stress. He was disturbing the class and the teacher called the office for help. When the call came in to the office I didn't know Mr. Crumrine was the intruder. He was not on my mind at all. I hurried down the outside walkway and was shocked at what I saw as I entered the classroom.

Standing inside the room was the biggest man I had ever seen in person in my life. He was huge. He was more than huge. He was World Wrestling Federation huge. He was at least six feet, six inches tall and weighed well over three hundred pounds, maybe more. He had long white hair that matched his long white, Santa Claus beard. But I knew he wasn't there to give out any gifts. He was a strange and scary sight for the students, the teacher and me. Once again, the intimidation factor was in full swing and it was swinging in my direction and I couldn't stop it. I had to stay there and do something. I was the principal.

He was very aggressive as he voiced his dissatisfaction and complaints against the teacher, the school and me. It didn't take long for him to arrive at his hidden agenda.

"I pay your salary to teach my child, not to send him to the office. I pay you to teach him the right things, not this Martin Luther King crap. What about teaching our children about Robert E. Lee and the real heroes in history. He ain't writin' no paper about no black man. My lawyer will contact you in the mornin'. I've had teachers fired before. You'll be next. I am a close friend of the mayor and the school superintendent. You're next."

I don't know why I let that monster of a man talk as long as I did. I guess I was scared. I came to my senses and it was my turn.

"Excuse me sir, but you can not be here like this. Please leave or the police will remove you from the building." He turned his attention and his massive body toward me. My heart went wild in my chest as he moved toward me. I knew he could hear my heart pounding, because I could hear it. He loomed even larger as he came closer to me.

"I'll bet you're Reynolds, the big clown in charge of this circus." I found a little courage.

"You'd win that bet, sir. Now, please leave the room like I asked you."

"Oh, I'll leave, but it's time you and me had a talk. The school superintendent told me to call him if you gave me any trouble. I'll call him from your office if I need to."

I knew right away I had just encountered the number one intimidator on the earth. People who lie to scare others are the most dangerous of all. You can't beat people who say anything they want with no consciousness or concern for consequences. He scared me as much as any one before him and maybe even more than any of the others I had faced.

He wore denim overalls, like so many huge men seem to wear. When you're that big I guess you have to find ways to dress for comfort. He also had over three hundred pounds of body odor. Maybe it's hard to smell good when you're that big. I hadn't seen it at first, but as he moved toward the classroom door to leave with me I noticed he had a wooden cane to assist him. The walk to the office was slow and we did not talk. He labored as he walked and by the time he sat down in my office he was breathing heavily and sweating like the pig he was. The odor that emanated from his massive hulk was even stronger in the confines of my small office. I was sorry I hadn't just made him leave the campus. I wasn't thinking clearly and I had already made a few mistakes in dealing with the Bullwhip Man. I had become an expert at recognizing the intimidating tactics so I wasn't surprised when he started his again.

"You're on the way out, Reynolds. You're not doing a very good job and everybody knows it." He really was sad, but comical at the same time. I had a feeling I was looking at the most insane parent I had ever met. Actually, I had no idea just how insane he was. I would soon learn more than I wanted to know.

"How can you allow this Martin Luther King crap on the walls? It's all over the school." I just stared at the insane fat man. "Where are the pictures of Robert E. Lee and Jeff Davis? They did more than King. Let's give them a day." I was so sorry he was sitting in front of me.

"And your wall of presidents is all wrong. There were two other presidents before Washington. Read your history. Schools never tell you about the real heroes." I had enough.

"Mr. Crumrine, this meeting is over. Please leave. I have no idea why you're here and your presence is a disturbance to me and the school."

"I pay your salary. You have to talk to me."

"No sir, I really don't. You have a nice day." I stood up and walked to the office door. For some reason he realized we were through and he did not continue. He grunted and wheezed as he struggled to get out of the chair, but said nothing to me. I was glad he was leaving. He moved slowly like before, but his direction was toward the exit. I briefly talked to the office staff about my encounter with Mr. Crumrine. I guess I needed to see friendly faces and hear friendly voices. There was always a good feeling when your fellow workers supported you and worked along with you. As we discussed the "huge one", another call for my assistance came from another classroom. A parent had entered a classroom and was yelling at the teacher. This time the intruder was in the new building. I was on my way. I wasn't sure how much more excitement I could take that day.

I turned down the long hallway of the new building to see Mr. Crumrine standing in the doorway of another classroom. He was giving his, "I pay your salary" speech to another teacher. I asked Mrs.

Frye to call the police as I passed her room and made my way to confront him.

"Mr. Crumrine, I have called the police and I will have you arrested if you are here when they arrive. Now, please get out of the building." He was red-faced, with anger. It was a scary sight as he stepped out into the hall to meet me. My throat went dry, but I had made a stand and scared or not, I would have to play it out. I was sorry I had allowed the problem to continue. I had no idea what was to come. All I knew was I wanted to hear those sirens coming in the distance, but I never did.

We stood eye-to-eye again. Perhaps not eye-to-eye, but we were looking at each other as he glared down at me. He surprised me when he lifted his cane and pushed the tip of it against my chest, like you might poke someone with your finger. It didn't hurt at all, but the idea of him thinking he could do such a thing to me sent all my professionalism out the window. As he held the cane up toward me I grabbed the end of it and jerked it out of his hand and with one motion, threw it down the hall. When the wooden cane hit the freshly waxed tile floor it slid the entire length of the hallway and didn't stop until it hit the wall at the far end of the hallway. I couldn't believe the distance it traveled. I think we were both in shock. I know I was. If cane tossing were in the Olympics, I could compete.

He held onto the wall to keep his balance. I knew he wanted to get his big hands on me, but we both knew he couldn't. I had the advantage and I liked the feeling for a change. I'm ashamed to say, I enjoyed watching him struggle as he worked his way down the long hall keeping contact with the wall to keep his balance. It took him forever to reach the cane and it was even more of a struggle for him to pick it up off the floor. I didn't care. I was sorry later that I didn't care, but that was later. He left and the police never came. I informed security about Mr. Crumrine's disruption of the school. I sent him a letter stating he was not allowed on the school campus and he would be arrested if he returned.

A few days after my confrontation with Mr. Crumrine he started a rumor about me in the neighborhood. He told people I had been a member of a military organization of assassins in Vietnam. He said we were both in the organization and he had me thrown out and that was why I hated his children. He also said I had told him I would get even with him and I was using the children to do so. He said I had changed my appearance, but he knew I was his old enemy from the past.

When no one believed his story he transferred his children to another school where he was arrested for causing a major disturbance in the school. Were people crazy, or what?

Crack Willie

I sure liked Willie. He reminded me of my two brothers when they were little. He had the same physical appearance they did and I loved that look. He had red hair and freckles. It was a great way to look. Willie was very nervous and he needed constant attention from his teacher or any adult around him. He wore penny loafers and white socks with his jeans rolled up once above the shoe, forming that fifties two inch cuff. I enjoyed seeing him during the day. Even when he was having a bad day, I still liked being with him. When the class was allowed to bring in their favorite music tapes for listening, most of the students brought in tapes by Michael Jackson, M.C. Hammer and Guns 'n Roses. Willie would bring in Jerry Lee Lewis, Fats Domino and Elvis. Willie was truly a child after my own heart.

Willie was an exceptional education student in one of our emotionally handicapped classes. He had been sexually and physically abused and his everyday coping skills were very weak. His teacher, Ms. Burke, was a saint and had a gentle and caring way with children. It was a pleasure to work with her and see the way she handled the students.

Willie would bring Valentine cards in for the entire class, open the door for his teacher, and "yes sir" you to death. He would also throw food in the cafeteria, cry at the drop of a hat, talk about "ya mama" and share his lunch with anyone at the table. He walked to a different drummer than most others in the world around him. He could make you mad, but he was easy to like.

It had been a tough week for Willie. He was unhappy with his father's change in work schedule and now Willie had to go to his aunt's house after school each day. For some reason he was upset with the new arrangements and he was taking his anger out on his teachers, classmates and anyone who came near him at school. He had spent most of the week with me in my office, as I was trying not to send him home. When he purposely threw crayons at Ms. Burke, his reign of terror had to end. Willie stood in my office once more and as usual he was nervous.

"Willie, I've tried to work with you this week, but I think you have run out of chances. I think you need to go home until you can act like you're supposed to." Willie always had excuses and was never at a loss for words. It was never his fault. That day was no different.

"Can I tell you why I'm so bad?" Even though I knew he would have an excuse, his question and sad tone surprised me. I was all ears.

"Sure Willie, I would like to know." His head was down.

" Everybody calls me names."

"Willie, you call people names everyday. And you've been called names before. Why is it such a big deal now?"

"They call me crack baby and crack boy and crack Willie. I ain't no crack baby."

"Willie, that's nothing. You know you're not any of those things. Don't pay attention to that silly talk."

"I don't like it. It embarrasses me."

"Willie, do you use crack?" He looked up and was surprised at my question.

"No sir."

"I've met your mother and father and they don't use crack, do they?" He didn't like that question.

"No sir, they don't use crack! That's crazy, Mr. Reynolds." He was angry with me.

"Then why do you care what they say if you know it isn't true?" He gave me a puzzled look.

"Mr. Reynolds, I don't know what you're talkin' about. All I know is every time I bend over the crack of my butt shows and then they call me "crack baby". After I recovered, I called Willie's mother and he wore suspenders the next day.

Southern Breakfast Belle

I will always hope in my heart the next incident I share with you was not my fault. Some have said it was entirely my fault, but you will see why I don't want to take the blame for the outcome. I was very concerned about a comment I heard from one of our older and more experienced teachers. A real veteran, if you will. She was referring to some of her first grade students. The comment was: "Those little niggras only understand a good pop on the butt." She said, "niggra" not Negro. I guess it was her own personal slang, but I didn't like it at all and I called her to my office at the end of the school day. It is another duty that falls upon a principal, to be sure all the children are treated equally without prejudice by our faculties.

Ms. Lane had been teaching for twenty-eight years, had two more left to retire and had been voted teacher of the year in three different schools during her career. She was a true southern bell and it came through clearly in her mannerism. It was obvious she considered herself untouchable and above reproach in her role as a teacher. Her evaluations had been excellent and her character had never been questioned. When she sat down in my office she was cool, calm and controlled. She knew I could do nothing to her, but I knew she was a racist and she taught in our school each day. I just wanted her to understand I knew what was in her heart and I didn't approve. I didn't care if it mattered to her or not, it mattered to me, not only as a principal, but also as a person and I wanted her to know.

"Ms. Lane, please do not refer to the black children in this school as "niggras" and I hope you are not popping them on the butt as a means of discipline." I was surprised when she merely smiled at my statement. I probably shouldn't have been but I was. She really didn't care. Sometimes I hate those tenure laws.

"Is that all, Mr. Reynolds?"

"I guess it is, Ms. Lane. Thank you."

I was still glad I let her know how I felt. Perhaps she would think twice before she made her remarks again. I didn't know what our relationship would be after the short conversation and my request to her. I never had the chance to find out. The next morning she dropped dead at the breakfast table. She was found face down in her cheese grits.

Spelling The Word

I was very curious when Mrs. Highsmith told me I had a long distance phone call. When I answered the phone it was a Mr. Long, the principal of a school in Michigan. He was concerned about a family he had been working with for about three months. He told me he had to have a young man named Alvin Lester arrested for abusing his family. Not only had Mr. Lester hurt his wife and his stepchildren, but he had also abused an infant. Lester was in jail and his family was staying in a shelter for battered women. The school's parent organization was giving the family money so they could return home and get away from Lester. Mr. Long asked me if I could assist them when they returned. I told him we would do what ever we could and that we knew the family well. At the end of the conversation Mr. Long said he was sorry I would have to deal with the Ludes again, but he was glad they were leaving his school. I understood perfectly. I couldn't believe they were headed our way again.

After the phone call I made one of our parents mad when she came into my office and said her son had learned the "F" word at school and she was very upset about it. I told her we had never had the "F" word on a spelling test so he must have learned it somewhere else. She told

me she considered my reply an uncaring, smart remark and she said she
was calling the school board to report me.

The Watch

Kevin stood in front of my desk holding his broken watch. His friend, Larry, stood next to him. It was a great looking sports watch and I was sorry the wristband was broken. Larry admitted he had broken the watch and I could see he was sorry. He said his father would buy a new band and fix it at home. He would return it in a few days. Kevin agreed and told me he didn't want his mother to know it had been broken. The two boys were good friends and both fifth graders. I allowed them to make their own decisions about dealing with the watch. Larry took it home. It was just another one of my administrative mistakes.

I didn't hear anymore about the watch for a week or so. In fact, it never even crossed my mind again until Kevin stopped me in the hall and told me Larry had not given his watch back. I wanted Kevin to know I was interested so I went to find Larry.

When I questioned Larry about the watch, he said it was fixed and he just kept forgetting to bring it with him in the mornings. He would return it tomorrow. It seemed reasonable enough and I could do nothing but agree. Kevin was happy and satisfied with the good news. Sometimes as adults we don't think about how important some things are to children. I should have taken care of the watch situation sooner.

It happened again and I forgot about the watch until Kevin approached me again almost a week later. No watch, as yet. I called Larry to my office and he made the same agreement as before. He would bring the watch to me first thing the next morning. I agreed once more. I wrote myself a note and the first thing I did the next morning was find Larry, but he had no watch.

"Larry, how do you get home in the afternoon?" I had to do something about the watch. It wasn't fair to Kevin and I should have helped him. Larry put his head down.

"My dad picks me up, why?"

"You know why. Come get me after school. I need to talk to your father about the watch. Kevin trusted you and so did I." The look on Larry's face was strange and it was obvious he didn't want me to talk to his father.

"Larry, you're a good young man here at school and this isn't like you to not keep your promise. Now, what's the problem with the watch?" I could see it was a struggle for Larry to talk so I gave him time to collect his thoughts. "You know you have to give the watch back to Kevin, don't you?" He agreed with a nod of his head and took a deep breath.

"Mr. Reynolds, my dad won't give the watch back. He really likes it and he's been wearing it to work." I didn't want to believe what Larry said, but I knew it was true and it wasn't Larry's fault. I couldn't wait to meet his father.

I made sure I was in the front circle drive of the school at dismissal time. I saw Larry walking from the fifth grade area. He walked to a beautiful late model black Ford Mustang and climbed into the passenger's side. The cars in the circle were moving slowly so I knew I would be able to reach the Mustang before they left the driveway. I walked to the driver's side and the car stopped.

It was easy to see Larry's father was a big man. I never seemed to have problems with the little men. He had long black, Indian-type hair and wore a tank shirt, showing his muscular chest, arms and tattoos. I really hadn't planned my approach and wasn't sure what to say. I wish I had thought about it more than I had.

"Excuse me sir, I'm Bill Reynolds, the principal here." I didn't like saying I was the principal as my own introduction, but sometimes it was needed. "I really need your help with a situation we have and I need a minute of your time."

"Sure what's the problem?" I thought his response was rather pleasant. Things were going quite smoothly.

"Well, I don't know if it is a problem or not, but Larry broke another student's watch a few weeks ago. He told me he would get it fixed and I let him take it home. In fact, he said you would fix it. Larry has not returned the watch and I thought you could help us."
He didn't bat an eye.

"No, I don't remember fixin' a watch or even seein' a watch." He looked at Larry, who had his head down. "What's this about a watch you broke?"

Larry said nothing and for a moment I was disappointed at the thought Larry had not told his father about the watch. I did feel sorry for Larry and I didn't want him to be punished for his mistake. I did, however, have to do something for Kevin. He had been the real loser so far, even if Larry had to take the punishment. I'm sure Larry had good intentions at first, but something went wrong and now he had to fix it. His father interrupted my thoughts.

"If I see it, I'll send it back. What does it look like?"

Then the vision hit me like a ton of bricks. I hated that sad excuse for a father. I couldn't believe he was sitting there talking and lying to me with the watch on his huge tattooed arm. Just like Larry told me. I was angry and lost. I know I was shaking, but I didn't care.

"It looks exactly like the one you are wearing on your wrist, right now." He was cool and calm as he looked down at the stolen item.

"This watch? Larry gave me this watch for Christmas. It's a great watch." Larry didn't look up, he couldn't. I felt his discomfort and shame. I wanted to jerk the watch off of his arm even if it meant breaking the band again and most likely, getting the beating of my life. I would fix it this time myself. I couldn't just let him drive away.

"Sir, I really can't believe you are going to keep that watch. Please tell me you're joking and you fixed the watch for Kevin." The thief was red-faced mad and he was not joking about the watch. My heart raced in my chest again, but I didn't care either. It was intimidation time and it was his specialty. He talked to me with clenched teeth, a sure sign of anger in most circles of civilization.

"You're sure this is the same watch, are ya? And there's no way Mr. Principal could be wrong?" I wanted to tell him that even Larry, his own son, knew it was the same watch, but I couldn't do that to Larry. He had enough to deal with without me adding to his problems. He had to live with that low-life.

"It really looks like the same watch, sir. In fact, I'm sure it is. I'm just sad and disappointed you have decided to keep it. Especially at the expense of a child." He was a thief and intimidator.

"Don't make me get out of this car, Mr. Principal. You won't like me if I have to get out of this car." I couldn't help myself as I fell to his low level. Where was Mrs. McWilliams when I needed her? Probably saving someone else.

"I don't like you already, in or out of the car." I could tell he was surprised at my comment, but not as surprised as I was. I really wanted to take it back, but it was too late for that. He was actually lost for words for a moment and as he hesitated, I added to my foolish moment.

"If you're getting out of the car, go park it out of the way and I'll be right here." I don't know what made me talk like that. I needed Mrs. McWilliams to bring my professionalism back to the surface. I was just so tired of the intimidation tactics I faced each day. It was a way of life for so many people. I moved away from the car and onto the sidewalk. His look of anger intensified as he drove slowly around the circle. I watched for him to pull into one of the parking spaces, but to my surprise he passed them all. He was gone and the watch with him.

I was proud of my personal stand, but I was disappointed in myself for losing the watch. Were people crazy, or what?

Death of A Young Astronaut

Mike loved our Young Astronaut Program. He was active in all aspects of the club. He was a good student and a good brother to his sister, Karri. She was absolutely beautiful, a future fashion model, no doubt. They were well-mannered, respectful and fun children. Children are supposed to be fun.

The first time Mike passed out at school, we knew something was very wrong. I don't know why, but I knew it was serious as I talked to him in the school clinic while we waited for his mother to pick him up. Within weeks a tumor was removed from his brain. He was schooled at home for five weeks as he recovered from the operation. His mother, who I had only seen one time when she picked him up that day, was struggling with him at home as she watched his health failing slowly. Somehow, she and the doctor decided Mike needed to be in school and be treated as normal as possible. They were hoping his spirits would be lifted around the other students and the everyday activities of the school setting. It would also take the strain off his mother. I didn't know if being in the caring business makes us the answer to any and all the problems our families face. There was so much more to our schools than education; too much more.

Mike's mother abused me on a daily basis, as he could not cope in the school setting. His medication made him sick when he moved around and he spent most of his time at school sleeping in the clinic. The school staff, as usual, worked very hard to keep Mike in school, but it was too much to ask of them. We always ask too much of our teachers. They cannot be everything to everybody. Ms. Elkins worked with Mike each day to help him stay in school, but it was just too much for us all. It was easy to see why his mother wanted some help, but I don't know if we should have been it.

As parents we know when your child hurts, you hurt. I was sure his mother felt helpless during that awful time. I became concerned for her when I started seeing her everyday. It was obvious she was a cocaine user. I had become very good at spotting the drug abusers. The combination of the stress and the drugs had taken its toll on her.

She arrived at school one afternoon so she could walk Mike and his sister home. I saw her standing at the bicycle rack and I approached her. I asked her about keeping Mike home and we would send a teacher to her house. He could be hospital homebound.
She didn't like my suggestion and became very defensive. She started yelling at me.

Her husband had left them and she felt she was going crazy. She began to cry and her voice grew louder and louder as her frustration and anger poured out of her. Then, to add to my awkward situation, she began beating on my chest with her closed fists. It was just like the ladies do in the movies. As she pounded on me, she cried and talked to the rhythm of her fist.

"I...can't...take...much...more...of...this.." She wasn't really hurting me, but I did move back away from her contact. Mrs. McWilliams, once again, rescued me and took her into the school building to calm her.

We attended Mike's funeral just before the end of the school year. He was dressed as a young astronaut. It was a sad moment for us all. Mike's sister, Karri, held my hand at the gravesite. It was a touching moment for me and an honor having her think enough of me to do that. Children are always full of surprises. You just never know. Karri would become a victim of the tragedy. Her life, personality and attitude would change drastically. I would also have the opportunity to hold her hand again.

Mike's death and the turmoil of her home and family life changed Karri's attitude completely. There were rumors of her parents fighting, her mother using cocaine on a regular basis and even a story about her mother being arrested and losing her job. Kerri started wearing heavy make-up at school and short skirts. She was sent home a number of times for her improper attire. She became disrespectful and a problem in the classroom and around the school in general. It was sad for me to see that beautiful child have her life change so drastically.

There seemed to be no way for us at school to stop or even slow down her sad transformation. The sweet child, who held my hand at her brother's funeral, now, cursed teachers like a wild child of the streets. I had no idea that morning it would be the day I would hold Karri's hand again. This time it would be very different from the day we buried her brother.

Your Mama

One of the Hamilton brothers, I never could tell them apart, handed me an envelope and walked away from me without a word of explanation. It contained a strange note, I assumed, from his father.

"I will be at school at 4:00. Don't leave."

Hamilton

Now, I really needed to know more about such a note. I was hoping to be on my way home at that time, not waiting on a parent. I had talked to Mrs. Hamilton a number of times about the boys' behavior, but nothing major. I called them to my office. I called both boys because I had no idea which one had delivered the note. They really looked alike.

"Which one of you brought me the note this morning?" The one on my right raised his hand like he was in class. We always raise hands in elementary school.

"Which one are you?"

"Adam."

"Okay Adam, do you know why your dad wants to see me? And why so late in the day?" Adam had the answer.

"He always waits on us at the bus stop near the apartment. He's going to ride the bus back to school. We don't have a car."

"Why is he coming to see me? The note makes me think he's mad about something." Adam looked down and his voice faded.

"He is mad at you." Even though he spoke softly, I heard what he said.

"Do you know what he's mad about?" Adam looked up at me and again had the answer.

"Cause you been talkin'bout our mama." I was once again sad and amazed. I didn't continue with the questioning. I let the boys go back to class. I had a note ordering me to stay at school and wait for an angry parent. It was typical as the intimidation tactics continued. I don't really know why, but I decided to take the offensive posture for that encounter. I boarded the bus after school and rode home with the Hamilton brothers. You talk about crazy. I had gone a little nuts myself.

As the bus approached the bus stop, I saw a group of adults waiting for their children to arrive. Only one man stood with the group, the others were women. I could see it was Mr. Hamilton. The boys looked just like him. It was down right scary how easy it was to pick him out as dear old dad. The bus stopped, the door opened and I was the first one to get off. He was talking to one of the ladies and had his back to me as I stepped up behind him.

"Mr. Hamilton, you sent me a note. You wanted to see me? I thought I would save you a trip to the school. Did you need to see me about something?" He was shocked to see me and his face said it. His upper lip quivered and he stuttered with his reply.

"Mmmy..my wife wrote that. Sss..she wanted to talk to you." I knew he was lying, but I could also tell he was shaken by my presence and aggressive tone. He was intimidated and I liked it. I would feel bad about my unprofessional action later. I got back on the bus for the ride back to the school. My shallow victory would only last about a half mile.

The Circle

The bus turned the corner and we were only a few blocks from the school. I noticed the bus was slowing down so I looked up, interrupting my thoughts about Mr. Hamilton. I could see a large group of people standing in an open area next to the road. The crowd was a mixture of young people and adults. They formed a circle and they were shouting and moving around. Something strange was going on. The bus moved slowly by the crowd. The driver and I both sat high enough on the bus to see into the circle. I thought perhaps two men were fighting, but I could not see anyone at first. I even thought maybe they were watching two dogs fighting, perhaps pit bulls. The neighborhood was full of the vicious dogs.

I can't explain the feeling that took over me when I saw why the crowd had gathered. Two young girls were fighting in the middle of the circle. Not one adult in the crowd made any effort to stop the action. They only cheered and encouraged the girls to continue. I was sick to my stomach as I watched. Once again I didn't want to believe my eyes. My disgust intensified when I recognized one of the fighters. It was Kerri. Her little life had sunk to being a fighting dog in a ring. I didn't know the other girl. She was bigger than Kerri and seemed older.

The bus stopped and without thinking, I jumped off the bus and pushed my way through the crowd and into the circle. Some one had to stop the insane spectacle. I pulled Kerri away from the other girl. They were both bleeding and had torn clothing. I held Kerri and moved her further away from the other girl. I could tell they both had no desire to continue. An ugly woman stepped out of the crowd and moved toward me.

"Let my daughter go. This ain't none of your business."

I knew right away the ugly woman standing in front of me and up in my face was not Kerri's mother. I also knew I could not stand by while two children fought like dogs in the street for the pleasure and entertainment of the "Sin City" crazies. I moved Kerri toward the bus and did not respond to the ugly lady.

"Kerri, get on the bus and we'll call your mother to come get you at school." I knew Kerri was relieved to have me there and she took my hand as we moved to the bus. We moved past the ugly woman and I couldn't see what happened to the other fighter. She was lost in the crowd, but I was sure she was as relieved as Kerri. We were at the edge of the human circle with people standing close to us, but a short muscular man in his late twenties blocked our path. Perhaps, I was being punished for my action against Mr. Hamilton. I could feel Kerri's fear as she held my hand. I was scared, too. I tried not to show my fear, but I don't think I was very convincing. My fear increased when the young man stepped closer to us.

"Good fight, girl." He directed his evaluation toward Kerri. Then, I received the rest of his attention. "Maybe you can take her place in the circle." He was dead serious and I was dead scared. He had smelled fear before and when a dog like him smells it, he has to continue. It's in the code of the true intimidator. "But, queers like you don't get in a circle like this, do ya?"

Now, for some reason, somebody always calls me a queer. I'm not sure how I project that thought, but it comes far too often. I did wear colorful shirts and ties, even pink shirts now and then. I never knew why I was called names, but I did know I was tired of it and I was tired of being afraid. I don't know why, but I just couldn't help myself as I fell to another very low level and once again said something real stupid.

"I tell you what. I'm going to take this child back to the school and call her mother to come get her. Then, I'll come back here if you'll get in the circle with me."

I couldn't believe those words came from my lips. I wanted to take them back, but it was too late. The crowd was quiet, waiting for his response. Kerri and I moved past him. I was surprised when he didn't say anything to me. He may have and I just hadn't heard him. Kerri never released my hand as we walked up the three steps of the bus. I left Kerri at school with Mrs. Highsmith, trying to call her mother.

I was nervous about the circle that awaited me, but I was also sick of the fear and intimidation I felt each day. Once again, professionalism took a back seat. The sight of those adults cheering for the two young girls flashed in my head. My stomach burned with fear and anger. Enough was enough in "Sin City". I went back to the circle.

My mouth was dry and my heart was pounding as I drove to the open area. I was surprised to see there was only a small group of adults standing together and not even enough to form the big circle I had seen before. I scanned the group for the short muscular man I had challenged. He was not there. I was relieved as I stopped the car near the small group. I opened the car door and stepped out. All eyes were on me. I heard that Clint Eastwood music in my head.

"Tell him I came back."

One of the men in the group surprised me with his comment. "You just won me fifty bucks, mister. I bet 'em you'd come back. You're all right." I guess that was a compliment. I went home.

The Pointer

I hadn't thought about the Mexican and Richard for a number of weeks until Detective Moneyhun called me one morning. He told me the police in Syracuse, New York had found the Mexican. He and his wife were in a bus station and he got into an argument with another man. The man was the aide to the mayor of the city. During the confrontation the Mexican stuck a knife in the aide's throat. He was arrested and was facing possible prison time for the assault. The aide did not die, but was badly injured. I was sure if the Mexican had been able to catch me he would have broken my legs.

That same morning, I didn't know what to tell one of our parents, Mrs. Hall, when she told me she was on the verge of killing her son, Cecil. He was a fifth grader and he had become the "pointer" for a gang of drug dealers who had taken up their illegal trade in the apartment complex near the school. The pointer, usually a minor, was the one who pointed out the dealer to the potential buyer. This was done so the dealer did not make the actual exchange of the money or the goods. He could only be arrested for possession, the lesser offense, but not for selling. A child caught with the money or the drugs would not be treated as an adult. Cecil must have been one of the best pointers. Mrs. Hall said he would be gone for days at a time and the dealers protected him at the apartment complex. He was treated with respect and was making as much as six hundred dollars a week. Cecil was eleven years old. It was hard for her to refuse such money coming into the house, but she was trying hard not to give in to the easy drug money. The Miami Boys had even threatened her and told her to leave Cecil alone, or he wouldn't have a mama.

Mrs. Hall came to me because she had fought with Cecil the night before when she held a large kitchen knife to her son's throat. It was a day of knives to the throat for me. She really thought she was going to kill him. The horrible thought of killing her own son hurt her deeply and she needed help for them both. She cried as she told me about the sad confrontation with her only son.

"He said he was leaving for a few days. When he tried to leave I hit him with my fist and he fell to the floor. He was surprised I hit him so hard. I took the knife off the counter and held it to his throat. I told him I had brought him into this world and I would take him out. It really scared him and he didn't move. I was so glad I stopped. I came so close to killing my baby boy. I'm ashamed of myself."

She made him go to his bedroom and she went to bed. About an hour later she went to bed and felt bad about locking her bedroom door, but she was afraid he was angry enough to hurt her. Cecil was gone in the morning.

He was arrested a few days later and did not complete the fifth grade with us. Cecil spent two years in Tampa, Florida, in a detention center for young criminals. During that year at school, two more of our fifth graders wrote essays about what they wanted to be. They wanted to be a "pointer".

One Tooth

Late one Friday afternoon, I was the last one to leave the school. The parking lot was empty except for my car and another car parked near the garbage dumpster. There was an old man, probably in his late seventies, looking into the large metal container. I thought he was talking to himself as he worked through the garbage. I was surprised when he reached into the dumpster and pulled out a skinny little blonde-haired boy. The child was absolutely filthy. No child had ever been dirtier than that boy at that moment. The old man took some items out of the child's hand and threw them into the back seat of a rusty green station wagon. They drove away.

On Monday morning Ms. Keller, one of our second grade teachers, brought a child to my office. He was Danny, a new student. I recognized him right away as the little boy in the dumpster on Friday. I also recognized some of the dirt still on him. The teacher was concerned with his appearance and left him with me in the office. We tried to contact someone to help us with Danny, but there was no home phone and no emergency number. Upon further investigation we found that Danny had a severe case of head lice; a very contagious condition we were familiar with and something we didn't need. We had fought the Sibble family plague of pestilence and we didn't need a new carrier.

Danny sat in the clinic for the first hour of the day until I decided he
would take a bath. We had that good old bathtub and we had all the
soap and head lice shampoo we would need. He bathed himself and I
treated his hair. He was a great looking boy without all the dirt. He
had to feel better. He went to class.

Danny became a terror at school. He was very smart and capable,
but he was not interested in school at all. He was rude and
disrespectful. He ran away on a weekly basis. We could always find
him hiding in the dumpster. It was a familiar place for him and I guess
he thought it was a good place to hide. The old man I had seen with
Danny was his grandfather, Mr. Timmons. Danny had an older sister,
Mary, in the third grade and a younger sister at home. Mr. Timmons
started coming to school each morning and would stand in the cafeteria,
watching Danny and Mary eat the free school breakfast provided for
the welfare children. Mr. Timmons smelled so bad it was actually
nauseating to be near him. All of his teeth had rotted down to the gum
line, except for one big front tooth. The lone tooth was in a serious
stage of decay, but it still had a little time left before it fell out too. He
looked like the puppet, Kukla, from the show Kukla, Fran and Ollie.

To add to his body odor, he smelled like liquor. He seemed to be
under the influence of alcohol most of the time, but he was able to hold
a conversation if you could stand being near him long enough. Some
true alcoholics can drink throughout the day and still remain normal in
some ways. It was plain to see Mr. Timmons was a true alcoholic.

Our troubles at school began to become more disruptive, with
Danny and Mary causing major disturbances. Mr. Timmons was no
help at all and HRS was alerted to the sad and neglected lives of the
children. An investigation gave us some strange information.

Mr. Timmons was the children's legal guardian, but not their blood
grandfather. Mr. Timmons' stepson was their father. The father was in
a home for the mentally disturbed. Their mother was mentally retarded
and after the third child, Vickie was born, the mother did not return
home from the hospital. No one knew where she went. She had been a

missing person ever since. Mr. Timmons had a wife at that time, but she had died. He was raising the three children alone. It wasn't long before Danny and Mary were tested and placed in our emotionally handicapped classes.

During the next two years we worked with the strange dysfunctional family. The little sister Vicki was as disturbed as the other two. They were the first family to receive food baskets during any holiday. We continued to bathe Mary and Danny at school when it was necessary. Danny stopped hiding in the dumpster. I had to call HRS and keep them involved from time to time.

On one occasion I called and reported that the children had been badly bitten in their beds by fleas. When I saw the hundreds of fleabites that had been scratched until blood was drawn, I had to report the sadly neglectful situation again. The HRS helped the children with medication. It was difficult for the poor, itching children to work hard at school when fleas were eating them alive at home.

The older sister, Mary, became very violent in her fifth grade year. She began to injure Danny while he was away from school. Danny would come to school with serious cuts and bruises. Danny told us it was Mary causing the damage. He said Mary always scratched him in his face when she got mad. He started locking his bedroom at night because Mary would wait until he was sleeping and then she would attack him. One time he said she was hiding under his bed and really scared him. You could see the surprise attacks were driving him crazy. He was injured a number of times and I asked HRS to look into the sad situation again. They made another home visit.

Mary's teacher, Ms. Burke, became concerned with her rapid, but misguided and premature maturity. She began to change physically and mentally. Mary started talking nasty with sexual overtones. Her language was obscene and she drew sexually explicit pictures during class. Mary's physical change was so drastic that Ms. Burke wanted to help her with her personal hygiene and work with Mary as puberty changed her. Good teachers always think of ways to help children.

Ms. Burke worked with Mary for a brief time before she decided to talk to Mr. Timmons and get his assistance at home. She wanted to be sure Mr. Timmons understood how important it was to encourage Mary to keep herself clean. He needed to know we had to have his help with Mary, as well as with the other children. Mary was responding to the attention from Ms. Burke in a positive manner and her behavior at school improved. After Ms. Burke met with Mr. Timmons she came to my office very upset and told me this bizarre story.

She met with Mr. Timmons to talk to him about Mary and how he could help at home. Ms. Burke offered her assistance as he listened. He said nothing at all. He only stared at her while she talked. She became uncomfortable as they sat together. Her discomfort came from the way he looked at her and the awful way he smelled. After she told him what she needed, she really didn't think he would follow up on any of her suggestions so she decided it was time to end the meeting. Mr. Timmons, however, was not ready for the meeting to end and he added to Ms. Burke's discomfort.

"I just don't want her to get no diseases or nothin'. There's a lot of VD out there." The first words out of his mouth set a new tone for the meeting. Ms. Burke became nervous with the subject matter he had thrown out to her.

"Sir, I don't think that's a problem for Mary at this time, do you?" He wanted to take it to another limit.

"You know how to check a woman for VD, don't ya?" Ms. Burke became defensive with his question and tone.

"Mr. Timmons, I really don't think that's a proper subject for you and me to discuss. I was just hoping you would help with Mary." Mr. Timmons would not let up and continued his nasty comments.

"I learned the technique in the army. I tried it and it works." Ms. Burke stood up and directed her rude visitor to the door of her classroom.

"Have a nice day, Mr. Timmons." He was determined to give his information to the young teacher.

"All you do is stick your finger in your ear and get some ear wax on it. Then touch the woman in her private area with your finger. If it burns her and she acts wild, she's got VD."

Ms. Burke said she thought she was going to throw up at his sick remark. She tried not to show any emotion, but she knew he could read her discomfort. It was a discomfort the nasty old man seemed to enjoy. Ms. Burke walked away from him and left him in the hallway. I could see she was shaken by the incident and the fact that she had to relate the story to me. I went outside to talk to Mr. Timmons, but he was gone. I knew I would see him in the morning at breakfast.

I decided to report Mr. Timmons' rude and strange comment to the HRS representative for our area who was familiar with the Timmons' family situation. Another home visit took place. I missed seeing Mr. Timmons the next day at breakfast, but I did approach him later and told him if he bothered or upset another teacher he would not be allowed on the school grounds. I could see his anger, but he didn't respond to me at all. In fact, he gave me the silent treatment for a week or so. He did continue to watch his children during breakfast. He would steal an orange or carton of milk now and then.

A few weeks later a student fell on Danny outside during a physical education class. His hip and leg were badly broken and he had to have the breaks pinned by major surgery. He was in a body cast for many weeks. It was another sad situation to add to Danny's woes. He was taught at home through our hospital homebound program for eight weeks and then returned to us for the last two weeks before summer vacation.

Danny healed over the summer and came back in the fall as a fourth grader. Mary went to the sixth grade at another school and little sister, Vicki, entered our kindergarten program. Grandfather still smelled awful and that one tooth in the front was still hanging on, but it was going fast.

The Ludes Return

It had been about a month since I had gotten that phone call from the principal in Michigan. I had actually forgotten about the possible return of the Lude family. I was talking to our bookkeeper, Mrs. Gilmer, in the main office when I turned and received the shock of the week. My heart started that familiar pounding and my stomach burned. I couldn't believe my eyes. Alvin Lester stood at the front counter of the office registering the three Lude children back into our school.

The first thing he did was tell a lie to our secretary, Mrs. Williams. He told her two of the children, Steven and Crystal, had been skipped forward to the next grade while they were in a school in Michigan because our school was so far behind. He said Tommy, who had been in the third grade when they left us three month ago, was now in the fifth grade. Just how crazy was this man? He was told we would have to call the other school to verify his information. He became angry and left the office. He did leave the three children with us. So much for the jails in Michigan.

After Mrs. McWilliams called the school in Michigan, Steven and Crystal returned to the same grades they were in when they left. Tommy was tested for exceptional education placement and we were able to move him out of the third grade and into the fifth, so he could be with children his own age and size. Tommy would go to the sixth grade at the end of the year and we would only have two of the Ludes at school the next year.

I was really surprised one morning when a man walked into the main office and introduced himself as Jim Lude. He had proper identification and we talked for about an hour. He had come from Connecticut and he was trying to talk his children into going back with him. So far, Tommy was the only one interested in his offer. I told him about all the problems we had faced with the children and the awful home life they had been subjected to. He had already met Alvin Lester the day before when Lester threatened him with a knife. The police were called and Lester was arrested. Mr. Lude asked me to help convince the children to return to Connecticut with him. He thought once the children were with him he would be able to keep them. I did not want to be involved in such matters. It was a good idea, but it needed to be an idea without me in it.

We were all pleased to hear later that Tommy Lude had gone to live with his real father and attend the sixth grade in Connecticut. Steven and Crystal stayed with their mother and stepfather, Alvin Lester. I made sure the two remaining Lude children had white teachers for the new school year so we could avoid any early confrontations. I didn't like doing that, but I considered it a preventive measure. The two teachers were not so pleased, but good teachers always come through.

Steven was an awful fifth grader. He made nasty comments to girls, little girls. He was disrespectful on a daily basis, stole from his teachers and classmates, and was no doubt, "public enemy number one" of the school. He was a despicable character and he made it almost impossible for anyone to like him. Even Mrs. McWilliams, who liked everybody, had her moments with Steven. I do have to say, she still made an effort to find positive moments with Steven. Good guidance counselors like everyone, no matter what. I think they take classes that teach them to like people. It's part of the job.

One day a mother allowed her son to bring a miniature rocking chair to class. It was made of wooden clothespins and varnished. The other students would use it as a model and make their own chairs to use as Christmas presents for their parents. The little chair was beautiful and a great idea for a holiday surprise.

Steven stole the model chair and sold it to a lady in the apartment complex behind the school for a dollar. When I heard about Steven's latest crime against mankind, I just couldn't let him get away with another despicable deed. I went to his classroom and took him out of class. I made him take me to the lady's apartment and gave him a dollar to purchase the rocking chair back from the lady. The woman who answered the door was very nice when I introduced myself and explained to her the story behind the little wooden chair. Steven hated standing there with me, but I didn't care. I was so grateful that the lady was understanding and cooperative about giving the chair back to us. As we walked back to school Steven told me he was going to tell his mother how I had taken him out of class and what I made him do. Again, I didn't care. I told Steven, if I didn't get my dollar back first thing the next morning, he would be cleaning cafeteria tables for the rest of the year. I wondered where he stole the dollar he gave me the next morning.

Mrs. McWilliams and I both noticed a strange transformation in the youngest sister, Crystal Lude. Her attitude at school had never been very pleasant, but her new attitude went far beyond disliking school or being unhappy. She became a street fighter, speaking slang and profanities with every word. All her classmates hated being around her because of the nasty comments she made each day. She started wearing make up and adult clothes. It was a strange look for a fourth grader.

Mrs. McWilliams counseled with Crystal and tried to return her to the little girl world she belonged in. Crystal, however, constantly talked to the other students about sex and drugs. She wrote nasty notes and threatened her classmates with bodily harm. Her racial comments caused fights in the school and in the street. We would hear stories about her fights away from school and how she was so absolutely fearless.

One day she auditioned for a spot on the "Putting on the Hits" talent show at school; a show where the students would lip-sync to popular songs and imitate the singer. Ms. Lott, the vice-principal, was responsible for screening the acts before they were picked for the big show. After Crystal's audition, Ms. Lott asked me to come and observe the act. I went to the stage in the cafeteria.

Crystal's act was interesting to say the least. I'm not quite sure how to explain her body movements, but she was very sexual as she sang and danced on the stage. The act was too provocative for an elementary school talent show and she was not selected for the program. It was rare for a fourth grade student to be so preoccupied with sex. Mrs. McWilliams continued to work with Crystal to stop the child's seemingly escalating preoccupation with sex.

My struggle with Alvin Lester calmed somewhat. We heard he was working for an air conditioning company and perhaps he didn't have the time to bother me at school. I was looking forward to Steven going to the sixth grade and Crystal being a normal fifth grader. It was spring again and we had survived another year with the Ludes. I had been verbally abused a number of times by the mother and Alvin Lester during the year, but that didn't really bother me much anymore. It was old hat for me and I just didn't care. It is sad what you can get used to, sometimes. I had no idea the next encounter with the Ludes would be the most disturbing of all.

Crystal arrived at the main office about an hour late for school that morning. Her clothes were wrinkled more than usual and her hair was tangled. She looked terrible and it was obvious something was seriously wrong. Crystal told this story to Mrs. McWilliams.

On her way to school she was walking in the parking lot of the Famous Amos restaurant near the school. A van drove up beside her and two black men jumped out of the van, forcing her into the back of the vehicle. One of the men drove the van while the other man raped her. And then, the two men traded places and she was raped again. After they raped her they drove the van back to the parking lot and dropped her off. Then, she had walked to school.

Mrs. McWilliams took her story seriously and contacted the proper authorities. The police were coming to talk to Crystal and take her to the hospital. As long as I live, I will never forget the conversation Mrs. McWilliams had with Crystal's mother. She called Mrs. Lude and told her we had reason to believe Crystal had been abducted and raped on her way to school and the police wanted her to go to the hospital. Mrs. McWilliams asked her if she wanted to come get Crystal or just meet them at the hospital? If she needed a ride Mrs. McWilliams would go get her. This was her unforgivable answer:

"I can't go right now. I'm taking my hairdresser test in about an hour. Can one of y'all go with her?"

There is no way to describe how I felt when Mrs. McWilliams told me what Mrs. Lude had said. We had just told that poor excuse for a human being that there was a strong possibility her ten-year-old daughter had been raped and she tells us she can't go with the child to the hospital. Mrs. McWilliams told the police about her conversation with Mrs. Lude. Mrs. McWilliams went to the hospital with Crystal and the police went to find the child's uncaring mother.

Mrs. McWilliams stayed at the hospital with Crystal until she was released. The child's examination revealed a serious vaginal infection and that she had been sexually active. It was not determined that she had been raped that day. Mrs. McWilliams brought Crystal back to the school and then took her home. We never did see her mother. Mrs. McWilliams would later help Crystal at school and be sure she used her medication. Mrs. Lude was more than happy someone else was taking care of her daughter's needs. I disliked Mrs. Lude and Alvin Lester more and more each day. Mrs. McWilliams took care of Crystal at school until she was clear of the infection.

Reporting Mrs. Lude to the HRS only brought on another visit from the agency. Her neglect was reported and recorded a number of times, but not much was ever done. We had a sexually active fourth grade child with stories of having been raped. There were facts to support that there was an insane mother and an abusive stepfather. And we were supposed to expect that ten year old to come to school and act normal. Were we nuts, or what? Mrs. McWilliams was the child's salvation.

About three weeks later Crystal told Mrs. McWilliams she was playing in an empty apartment when a black man came in and raped her. Crystal said she had told her mother and it made her angry this time. A report was made to the police and they searched the area for the man. Crystal's rapid maturity continued during the next few months. Mrs. McWilliams' efforts to slow Crystal's exit from childhood were commendable, but it was too late. It has been said in educational circles that we can't save them all. Crystal was not a fun child to have around, but Mrs. McWilliams never gave up. Guidance counselors have always amazed me.

We continued our struggle with the Ludes and Crystal became a fifth grader. Steven left that summer to live with his real father and his brother, Tommy. Crystal's last year with us was as tough as the other years. Her maturity was far beyond that of the other children and her prejudiced attitude caused many serious problems at school.

The abuse Crystal's mother was taking from Alvin Lester was taking it's toll on Crystal, too. She was very smart, but she did very little work in the classroom. When she did complete an assignment it was very good. Her home life preoccupied her and, therefore, had taken away her desire to work or study.

Mrs. McWilliams suspected Alvin Lester as the reason for Crystal's sexual advancement and activity. Crystal would not talk about it. One time, during a counseling session, Crystal did mention her mother had to make Lester leave her alone one night when he was drunk. She said her mother waited for Lester to fall asleep and then hit him in the head with a board. The next morning they told him he had fallen down the stairs and hit his head when he was drunk. Crystal thought it was funny, sharing that untrue secret with her mother.

An interesting addition to the Lude saga was that after Crystal left the elementary school and became a teenager, she was a guest, along with her mother, on the Montel Williams' television talk show. She was a teenager who was living with an older man although her mother disapproved. Were people crazy, or what?

I tried to call my friend Detective Moneyhun to say hello and tell him I was still the principal in Sin City. I didn't get to talk to Ralph. I was told he had injured his back while chasing a fleeing criminal. The injury was serious enough for surgery. During the surgical procedure it was discovered that Ralph Moneyhun had terminal cancer. My friend had died.

Sally Returns

    Sally Dalton had been going to another school for almost a year. I was walking to my car on my way home, when I saw a young girl standing near the gate to the parking lot. She stood straddling her bicycle. I didn't recognize her from where I was standing. She seemed older then the other students standing near her. I got into my car and drove to the gate. I had told Mr. Owens, our custodian, I would close and lock the gate when I left. I stopped and got out of my car to lock the gate behind me. The girl had not moved and she continued to watch me. When I closed the gate my heart began to race when I recognized my strange visitor. I was looking deep into the now real adult eyes of Sally Dalton. Perhaps, she was looking deep into my eyes. It was a strange moment for me. I couldn't believe my eyes, or her eyes.

    Sally looked awful. She was a miniature version of her mother. Her dirty hands made a chill run through my body. Sally was extremely overweight and the extra pounds had affected her facial features. She only stared and said nothing. I had seen that same stare before and I did not want to see it again. I honestly felt she was standing there so she could feel safe, if only for a minute. It was scary how much she looked like her mother. I took a deep breath and acknowledged the fact I did recognize her.

"Well, Miss Sally Dalton, look how grown up you are. I didn't know it was you until I got closer. My eyes aren't very good from a distance. How are you?" My stomach burned when she only continued her deep stare with those adult eyes. " Sally, you should come to see us soon. Mrs. McWilliams would love to see you." She smiled, but still had no words for me. "Sally, can Mr. Reynolds help you with something?"

I gave her time to answer as we stared at each other. She never took her eyes off me. It was as if she wanted me to read her thoughts without having to actually talk to me. She must have realized my struggle to communicate. In a soft low voice she found a touch of courage.

"No sir, I just wanted to see you." She rode her bike away.

Perhaps it is true, we cannot save them all, but in a "caring" business we must continue to try. Sometimes the teacher is the only friendly and encouraging face the student sees each day. It is a great responsibility to be the salvation of so many. Our schools are not creating the problems. The problems are coming to school. The teachers are doing all they can to solve them, but they are overwhelmed and outnumbered. Educators will keep trying to make the difference. It is the real reason we do what we do. It is the best "deal" for the money the American public has. I do love teachers.